PRINCESS OLIVIA

*Wherein an Optimistic Slip of a Girl Brings Sunshine
Into the Lives of Her Royal Parents, the Whiny King
and the Scolding Queen, and Outsmarts the Despicable
Count Carlos Maximillian von Dusseldorf (with two s's) and
His Magical Minion, the Mischievous, Poetical Georgette...
and What is a Hoop Snake Anyway?*

a novel by
Charles F. D. Egbert

Illustrated by Kathie Kellerher

Bunker Hill Publishing

To my wife Carol for her love and help, and to the littlest Egbert, our granddaughter Anneke Isabelle

www.bunkerhillpublishing.com
by Bunker Hill Publishing Inc.
285 River Road, Piermont
New Hampshire 03779, USA

10 9 8 7 6 5 4 3 2 I

Copyright text ©2013 Charles Egbert
Copyright illustrations ©2013 Kathie Kelleher

Library of Congress Control Number: 2013934781

ISBN 978-I-59373-147-2

Designed by Joe Lops
Printed in China

Chapter *One*

A long, long time ago, in the Green Mountain King-dom that is now called Vermont, there was a prin-cess named Olivia. She had dark brown eyes and long brown hair with bangs in the front and a ponytail in the back. She was a serious person. She lived with her father, King Horace, and her mother, Queen Cora. Their castle was set high in the green hills and deep in the dark forests near the tiny town of Ipswich that clung to the side of a hill across Beaver Creek. They had a marvelous view of Mount Ascutney.

The castle had once been grand. The beautiful gardens sur-rounding the castle had gone to weed and seed. Brambles and wild grapevines grew over the marble statues that lined the spa-cious terraces, and volunteer asparagus, violets, and dandelions grew where there should have been grass.

Even worse than the condition of the castle was the condition

of the Royal Bank Account. It was as empty as the pantry. The Royal Family suffered a great deal, and so did the farmers and townspeople of Ipswich. They asked, "Why us?" and, "What have we done to deserve this?" But they never asked, "Who is doing this to us?" Because they knew! Everyone knew that all the bad things that happened in the Green Mountain Kingdom were because of Count Carlos Maximillian von Dusseldorf who was a flatlander. Some Royal subjects even thought he was European!

One pleasant sunny day in summer, after a very meager lunch, King Horace went back to bed to nurse his ailments. Queen Cora tried to amuse Olivia with one of her stories about life on the farm near Tunbridge, where she lived before she met Horace. It was a good story about cows and horses and goats and sheep and how she had to feed them all and how difficult it was and how brave she had to be. As soon as she finished it she started to cry. Things were that bad.

Princess Olivia felt sorry for her mother and patted her hand. "I wish I could help you, Mother, I really do. I wish I could do something for you and Father." Her soft brown eyes were full of concern.

"Thank you." Queen Cora stopped crying, blew her nose, and went to look after Horace. Looking after Horace was a full-time job.

Princess Olivia went out to her bower. She liked to be alone there, especially on nice sunny days like this one. Her bower was near the orchard, beyond the formal gardens, and a mere stone's throw from the castle. It was surrounded by large sugar maple trees and a few popples, which people in the rest of the world call poplars. The leaves from the trees dappled the sunlight that danced across the soft green grass. Usually she played on her swing or sat quietly and enjoyed her solitude, but on this day she was morose. She didn't have any friends, and her head was full of worry. What would become of her? Would she ever have any adventures? Would she come to the bower every day until she was so old that she couldn't come anymore, and then have to sit in a rocking chair by a window in the castle and wait for the sun to set? She was very sad.

To cheer herself up, she decided to think about something else, and the first thing that came to mind was the poem that she'd written for Diane. Diane was the name she'd given to an imaginary little sister, and went like this:

> *I wish I had a little sister,*
> *We'd run and play and climb a tree,*
> *I know what I would like to call her,*
> *Diane, Diane, she'd be to me.*

Charles F. D. Egbert

> *We'd fill the world with raucous laughter,*
> *Just she and me, at lunch and tea.*
> *We'd dance and dance, forever after,*
> *All 'round and 'round—fantastic'ly.*

> *We'd talk all day in regal chatter,*
> *Of Dukes and Earls and Royalty,*
> *We'd board a ship and hoist the anchor,*
> *And sail the sea, the deep blue sea.*

That was as far as she had gotten. She had lots more to say about Diane, but choosing the right words took time.

"Do you know what else I'd like to have?" she said out loud. "A butler! Think about it! Wouldn't it be great to have somebody bring you a glass of lemonade whenever you liked, or clean up your room when it was a mess, or tie your shoes when you're too tired to bend over. Wouldn't that be great? I think I'd call him Binkerton. *The shoes, Binkerton, the laces are a bit loose,*" she said, putting her dainty foot forward. "*Thank you, Binkerton.*"

Her cheerful thoughts didn't last long. Soon she was thinking again about her poor parents. "If I could just do something to help them," she said to herself. "I know that they used to be rich and regal, but now, because of that horrid Count Carlos, they're poor and miserable."

She was about to plop down in the grass to figure out what she could possibly do to help her parents, when—YIKES— there, right there, where she was going to sit, was a SNAKE! That's right, a snake, a snake in the grass!

"Heavens to Betsy!" she shouted and jumped away. Then, when she'd looked at it more carefully, she said, "Oh, my good- ness! There's something wrong with it. It isn't wiggling like a normal snake. It's more like a huge ring."

Olivia knew, from her *Natural History of the Green Mountain Kingdom*, that it was a genuine Green Mountain Hoop Snake. She had read that they formed themselves into hoops to roll down hills, which was much better than slithering if one had a delicate tummy, especially if the ground was gritty.

"And, oh my," she said, observing it even more carefully, "he has swallowed his tail! Heavens to Betsy!"

She turned to the snake who, despite his tail problem, had a small but very pleasant smile, and said, "Good afternoon." She didn't know if he would respond. She listened carefully but all she heard was hissy-hissy.

Boldly, she put her ear nearer to the snake and said, "Could you speak a little louder, please?"

"Hissy-hissy."

"What was that?"

"Hissy-hissy," the snake repeated as she put her ear down even closer.

After a moment she said, "Oh, I'm fine, thank you, Sir." Then she listened again. "What? Oh, yes, I imagine it must be very difficult to talk when you have a tail down your throat. How did it happen?"

In order to hear him, she picked up the snake and was surprised that he was dry rather than slimy. She held the snake to the side of her head like a telephone and listened.

"You were going around a rock. Yes. And you saw something wiggling about, trying to run off. Yes. And each time you got closer, it moved away. Yes. So what did you do? You went for it? And you caught it? And that's when it started to hurt? Boy, I bet it did. And then you realized what you had done. And it tasted bad as well—I hadn't thought of that." The snake hissed on for a while, and then she said, "Well, why don't you try breathing through your nose?"

"Hissy, hissy, hissy."

"Oh, yes, allergies, I have them too, it's quite common here in the Green Mountains. I didn't realize that snakes had so many personal problems. Yes, of course. My name is Olivia.

And what would you like me to call you, Sir? What? Oh, all right—Mr. Snake, then." He was unexpectedly friendly, and she was delighted to have a new friend in the bower.

Mr. Snake was hissing again. "Really!" said Olivia, "That's a funny idea. Are you sure?"

"Hissy, hissy."

"Okay, if you say so." So she took Mr. Snake, put him over her head, and started to move her hips about in a circle, but he slipped to the ground. "It didn't work."

"Hissy, hissy, hissy, hissy."

"Oh, I see. Well, I'll try again." And this time she got him going, 'round and 'round. "Heavens to Betsy! This is fun." While she was giving Mr. Snake the whirl-around, she heard a cry in the distance.

"OLIVIA? OLIVIA!" It was her mother, Queen Cora, coming to see if she had put her umbrella up. She was angry and looked like a storm brewing.

"What are you doing now, Child?"

"I'm playing with Mr. Snake."

"YOU'RE PLAYING WITH WHAT?" she shrieked. Mr. Snake was going around so fast that she didn't even see that he was a snake.

"It's not a 'what,' Mother, it's a 'who.' It's Mr. Snake."

"A SNAKE! ARE YOU OUT OF YOUR MIND?" Queen Cora, despite having grown up on a farm, was afraid of snakes.

"No, it's all right, Mother, he's a friend. He won't hurt me."

"HOW MANY TIMES DO I HAVE TO TELL YOU NOT TO PLAY WITH SNAKES?"

"But, Mother, he's a nice snake and he won't hurt me because he has swallowed his tail."

"I don't care if he has swallowed an elephant, young lady, snakes are vicious, prehistoric creatures without any sense of propriety or good table manners, and, besides, they sting." She was getting older and beginning to mix things up.

"They don't sting, Mother, they bite."

"EVEN WORSE! Now then, I came out here to tell you something. YES!—JUST AS I THOUGHT—you don't have your umbrella up."

"I will, Mother, as soon as it starts to rain."

"YOU WILL PUT THAT UMBRELLA UP NOW! DIDN'T YOU HEAR THE THUNDER?"

"Yes, Mother."

"WELL, HOW CAN YOU ARGUE WITH THUNDER?"

Olivia had heard a soft rumbling noise coming from way

over near Lake Fairlee, but had paid no attention. She opened the stupid umbrella just to please her mother, and didn't miss a turn with Mr. Snake.

"There! Now you are prepared for any eventuality."

"Yes, Mother."

"Mercy, mercy, I'm going to get soaked."

"It's not going to rain, Mother."

"And where, may I ask, is your sweater?"

"My sweater has holes in it. There is more hole than sweater."

The mere mention of sweaters caused her mother to begin one of her "sermons," as Olivia called them, and while her mother scolded, Olivia continued giving Mr. Snake the whirl-around.

"Can you never stop with that thing?"

"It's fun."

"Fun? Is that all you can think about? When I was your age I had to work, sweep the floor, clean the house, mow the grass, feed the chickens, milk the cows, muck the stalls, shovel manure, slop the hogs, and . . ."

She stopped only because, unexpectedly, the King limped into the bower.

"Father, are you all right?" Olivia ran to him.

"Horace, you shouldn't have come all the way out here."

"Bother," he said, "I'm not feeling well."

"What is it, dear, your big toe again?"

"Yes, yes it is."

The King had gout and his main problem was his stupid big toe. He hated this! A real Green Mountain man would complain about his lower back or his tennis elbow or his trick knee; only a wimp complained about a big toe. But he was grateful that it was not his little pinkie toe, the one that said, "Wee, wee, wee, all the way home." That would have been totally mortifying. If only he had been wounded fighting a fire-breathing monster while trying to save a damsel in distress, or had been injured by an angry polar bear while protecting a stranded, elderly, Eskimo lady from an avalanche of snow and ice—something more along those lines—something he could be proud of and boast about.

Princess Olivia watched him hobble back to the castle. "I wish I could do something to help him. He's so sad and mournful all the time."

"That's nice of you, Olivia, but I don't think there's anything you can do."

"What about picking some blackberries? There's a patch near here. And we could make a pie."

"That's a nice idea, but don't go far, and whatever you do, KEEP AN EYE OUT FOR COUNT CARLOS MAXI-MILLIAN VON DUSSELDORF." She said this every day, about a hundred times every day.

"Yes, Mother."

Chapter *Two*

The mere mention of Count Carlos sent fear into the hearts of everyone in Ipswich, and word of his misdeeds flew from Buskirk and Readboro in the south part of the Kingdom, to Troy and Derby Center in the north. Everything that went wrong, every wart, stubbed toe, bloody nose, missing cat, or flea in the ointment was because of him and his Magical Minion. They were responsible for broken fences, stolen pies, and things that went bump in the night. Coughs, sneezes, sour stomachs, headaches, and all things that were beneath the dignity of Count Carlos were attributed to his Magical Minion. In the blink of an eye she could become a bird who snatched off your hat, a big puff of wind that slammed the door closed when there was no breeze stirring, or a tiny puff of wind that could blow out a match just as you were trying to light a fire. She could even set dogs barking at absolutely nothing, in the middle of the night.

The ominous presence of this dangerous pair had hung over the Kingdom for several years like yellow smoke from a smoldering pile of rubbish. They traveled together about the countryside and had last been seen on Easter day, first on the covered bridge in Taftsville and then, later, on the crest of a hill near Bridgewater, headed west toward the small village of Rutland. The silhouette of his round body pulling a cart was seen set against a sky turned orange with the setting sun.

Mr. Atwood, the hairdresser on Main Street in Ipswich, had seen the Magical Minion in the form of a witch with a wart on her nose. She had looked in the window of his shop and right after she'd gone, his glasses broke, his teacup walked off the table all by itself, and he dropped his scissors down the back of the dress of his most demanding customer, Lady Potwin, who then screamed at him and left with his best scissors poking uncomfortably into her ribs somewhere under her corset.

"I've never seen anything like this," he said, "the whole time I been here," by which he meant his whole life, because he still lived in the house where he was born.

And it was getting worse. Every day there was something new.

Ezekiel Washtubs had seen footprints and cart tracks in the snow near his barn and was certain that Count Carlos had broken in and milked his cows before dawn. "Had to be him," he railed. "Who else coulda done it?" A week later, three of his chickens were missing and the remains of a fourth looked as if it had been eaten alive, because of the feathers and bones thrown all about. He was appalled. "And it can't be nobody but him that'd do something like that."

And Hope Sew and her brothers all had problems. One day, Hope was walking in the woods, and when she stopped to look at a beautiful trout lily a huge branch fell from a tree and crashed to the ground exactly where she would have been standing if she hadn't noticed the flower. When she looked up, she saw a coal-black crow with a smiling face and knew it was really the Magical Minion.

That very afternoon, Ignorance, the oldest of Hope's seven brothers, fell out of a tree and landed on top of two of her other brothers, Prejudice and Ineptitude, and all three of them tumbled headlong into the pond. Greed and Detritus ran for help, and Despair stayed behind weeping while Attention-Deficit wandered around wondering what was going on. Thankfully, the Ipswich Volunteer Fire Department arrived at the last minute and rescued them. They all agreed, without a shadow of doubt, that these misfortunes were the work of Count Carlos and his Magical Minion.

At the farmer's market, Mr. Black, the chimneysweep, told everyone that his ladder had been pulled away from the chimney just as he was about to climb down. "I couldn't see 'em, but I could hear 'em laughing at me, dangling as I was by my fingers from the rain gutter."

Gingerbread Baker, the baker's wife, broke a tooth on a pebble while eating one of her husband's pies. The only thing that stopped her from konking him with a rolling pin was that he broke a tooth at the very same time. They weren't certain who had done these evil deeds, but they'd seen five-and-twenty blackbirds playing around just outside their window, and they knew that Count Carlos's Magical Minion was able to transform herself into anything, even five-and-twenty blackbirds.

Count Carlos Maximillian von Dusseldorf's voice was heard in the thunder, and his face was seen in the gale. No one knew exactly what he looked like, but each person had his or her own notion, and all were variations on "ugly."

"How could he be so evil?" Princess Olivia asked her father.

"I don't know. I don't understand," the King said sadly. "It's because of him that we are so dreadfully poor."

Despite all the hardship and suffering, the townspeople still believed they were rich. And, of course, so did Count Carlos.

When Olivia looked at her father's sweet, tragic face, she wanted, more than ever, to help him find a way out of the trouble he was in. If she could only think of something!

Chapter *Three*

I mmediately after the Queen warned Olivia in the bower, "YOU MUST WATCH OUT FOR COUNT CARLOS MAXIMILLIAN VON DUSSELDORF!" they heard a noise, a sort of bangle-jangle noise that stopped as soon as it started. Something in the forest had made a very strange sound.

"Shhhh," hissed the Queen, and she peered into the darkest depths of the forest.

"I don't hear anything," said Olivia. And neither did Mr. Snake, who was all ears, so to speak.

The Queen waved her to silence. "I heard a noise."

"Stop it, Mother, you're scaring me."

They listened together for several minutes, but all they heard was the buzzing of the bees in the evergreen trees.

"It's nothing, Mother."

"The world is a dangerous place, Olivia, and the only way I

can teach you about it is to tell you all the terrifying stories I've ever heard, and exaggerate them out of all proportion, so that you will get the idea and be careful."

"I'm always careful, Mother."

"Like playing with snakes? Do you call that being careful? I'd call it—well, never mind what I'd call it—not fit for a young girl's ears. Now then, which way is it back to the castle? I'm all turned around." The Queen had a very poor sense of direction.

"It's that way, Mother."

"Thank you. Oh me, oh my, the trials and tribulations of being someone's mother. I never dreamed it would be like this. Not only that, but I hurt myself this morning." She put her pointer-finger, which was overworked with wagging, into her mouth and sucked it like a lollipop.

"I'm sorry, Mother."

"Never mind being sorry, just be careful," she said and headed off in the wrong direction.

"It's that way, Mother."

"Thank you." Before she got to the end of the bower, she turned and warned Olivia one last time. "Don't forget to watch out for Count Carlos Maximillian von Dusseldorf!"

"I won't, Mother."

Chapter **Four**

 Count Carlos Maximillian von Dusseldorf had wandered into the forest by chance and was not far from Princess Olivia and Queen Cora when he heard his name mentioned. He stepped back and tried to hide behind a tree, or two trees, actually, because he was so fat.

He wore the clothes of a gentleman, a black swallowtail coat, a grease-spotted bow tie, spats, and a broken stovepipe hat that, from the look of it, might actually have been someone's stovepipe not too long ago. As to the reeking, malodorous stench that emanated from his person, he claimed that he cultivated it—to keep away the mosquitoes.

The Count had a strong accent. He rolled his *r*'s and gurgled his *g*'s and topped off his *t*'s with the tip of his tongue. He pronounced the word *bodom*, you know, like the "bodom" of the bed where your feet are, with two *t*'s—*bottom*. This was a very strange thing to do in the Green Mountains and he thought it gave him an air of superiority, but in reality it was as far from the truth as possible since he was dirty, disreputable, evil looking, and crab-like, all due respect to crabs. He was so hunched over that he had to bend his neck backward just to look forward to see where he was going. He traveled the trails and paths of the Kingdom always on the lookout for something to steal or someone to cheat, trick, or lie to.

His cart, really a cage on wheels, was designed especially for capturing children and other animals. It had a tattered pad on the floor and a torn blanket because that's where he slept. The cart had been painted in shades of green so that it wouldn't be seen in the forest where he spent much of his time hiding. It would have looked nice except that the Count was a slob and hung his disgusting personal belongings on hooks on all sides of the cart including the inside and the outside. There were muddy boots, an old pair of breeches, saucepans, an orange jerkin, various tools and sundry accoutrements particular to his trade—evildoing— not to mention old socks and ragged undergarments badly in need of soap and mending.

The most amazing part of the Count's little entourage, and I have saved it, like dessert, until last, was standing on two legs inside the cage. She appeared to be a bronze statue and had a gray-green cape thrown over her shoulders. Although Count

Carlos talked to her more or less constantly, she did not answer. Her face was expressionless, totally blank, even when the Count was saying something wildly exciting, as he was now.

"Yes, Yes, YES," he shouted in a whisper. "Heh, heh, heh." That was his evil, ugly laugh. "She's perfect! Just think of it, my little one, think how much she must mean to her mother and father, and just think, they're the King and the Queen! It couldn't be any better. Yes, Yes, YES. IT'S BEYOND MY WILDEST DREAMS! And I'm sure they have lots of money, I'm positive. All we have to do is catch her, leave a little ransom note demanding all their money, and then I will be rich, Rich, RICH, beyond my wildest dreams. And it will be so easy! Don't you think, my Pet?" To which the bronze statue didn't even shake her head. "Oh, yes, I forgot," said the Count. The bronze face, although it appeared to be dead or frozen, had pleasant enough, even youthful features, said nothing.

Out of a small, inside pocket, the Count pulled an extraordinary little hat, a marvelous concoction made of horse feathers, rabbit's fur, and bobcat leather, all stuck together with good strong, seasoned cobwebs. Now, of all the things the Count possessed, this hat was the most valuable. Not pretty, but valuable. Why was it valuable? Because it was magical! When he put it on the bronze statue's head, she was transformed into a high-spirited elf. When he set her free, her face beamed with joy, and she threw off her cape exposing an organza bodice with mauve polka dots, satin and lace, three-quarter-length sleeves with empire seaming, a scalloped, delicate, sheer, sweetheart neckline, a rose madder bodysuit with three kangaroo pocquettes, and a complex system of buttons and bows to keep it from falling apart. Her final instructions to the seamstress had been quite specific.

> *"And at my elbows and my toes,*
> *I'll have rows and rows of furbelows."*

She leaped into the air, and did cartwheels and somersaults, one after another. She was remarkably agile and possessed incredible personal beauty—beauty so intense as to make one stop breathing, at least for a moment.

"Georgette!" shouted the Count. "That's enough!"

She immediately stopped cavorting about, stood like a soldier at attention, and said crisply, "Yes, SIR." As a bronze statue she had been pretty, but now, animated by the magic hat, she was gorgeous.

"AT ease," shouted the Count. She relaxed and stood with her feet apart and her hands held smartly behind her back like a well-trained soldierette.

"What can I do for you, my Liege?" she asked, with a hundred-dollar smile on her pixie lips. "Something awful, I hope, something really egregious, with lots of blood and guts."

"Yes, my little one, heh, heh, heh, you are such a sweet little thing on the outside and so vicious on the inside—just perfect for my purposes."

"What shall I do, Sir?"

"I have a little project for you."

> *"Send me hither, send me thither,*
> *Send me now and do not dither.*
> *I am thine and twice divine,*
> *And, if thou wilt, I'll bring thee wine."*

"Wine's a nice idea," said the Count, "but no, we don't have time. And please, no more of that poetic blather."

> *"I've two rhymes more or three or nine,*
> *When you decide to sit and dine."*

"What on earth are you talking about? Dine on what?"

And then Georgette said in a very deep voice,

"The rhyme's the thing,
Wherein we'll catch the coffers of the King."

"Yes, exactly, my Pet, now you're getting the idea."

"Yes, SIR," she said and saluted again.

"Now listen, here's what we have to do. Can you see that girl over there?" He pointed through the trees toward the bower. "The one with the dark bangs and the pretty pink cheeks?"

"Yes, my Liege."

"We're going to catch her."

"Oh, boy, and have her for lunch?"

"Always thinking of your stomach, aren't you. No! We're going to catch her and take her across the swamp, and make the King give us lots of money to bring her back. Gazillions of dollars! And we'll be rich, Rich, RICH, beyond our wildest dreams."

"Shucks, I was hoping we could have her for lunch."

"But first we have to catch her," said the Count, rubbing his hands together, "and that's where you come in. What do you think? Do you have any small spells that you could use to lure her into my little cage? Something not too large and not too small?"

Georgette struck her "thinking" pose for several moments.

"I could hide up in a tree and drop a rock on her head when she came this way." Almost everything she knew about harming people came directly from reading books written by people who knew how to harm other people from their experience with war, slaughter, hunting, and other human pastimes. "The history of man," she liked to say, with a solemn but charming expression on her face, "is the history of man's inhumanity to man and other animals." She, as a non-human, thought she could improve on man's ideas along these lines, "but why should I? They've done such a good job there's no need."

"A rock?" said the Count. "Yes, I like that. But, no, we mustn't hurt her. The King won't pay for damaged goods."

Sweet Georgette struck another pose, even lovelier than the first, pensive this time, her head tilted at a delightful angle.

"I could dig a hole and put branches over the top and when she came along she would fall in."

"Yes, very good. But no, she's not an elephant."

"Or maybe I could build a little gingerbread house, entice her in, and then push her into the oven."

"No, that's been done before."

"I KNOW!" she cried, jumping up and down. "I'll become invisible like this." She closed her eyes and became invisible. "You can't see me now because I have my eyes closed."

This doesn't work for most people; I know because I've tried it myself. Just because you have your eyes closed doesn't mean that other people can't see you. I can't explain why exactly, but it just doesn't work that way. With Georgette, however, it really did work and she was invisible, totally invisible.

The Count looked this way and that. "Yes, yes, my Pet, very good, very good. Now where are you? Don't be a pest, little one."

She jumped about like a grasshopper. "Over here!" she shouted and jumped over his head. "Over here!" "Over here!" "Over here!" she called out, each time from a different place. She was quick and beautiful! Or, at least, would have been, if she hadn't been invisible.

"Yes, very good," said the Count, "your skills have improved indeed."

She wasn't quite finished playing, and suddenly, at least for the Count, she stomped on his toe. "Ha, ha, ha," she laughed merrily and ran around the cart.

"Ow," shouted the Count, cursing and holding his stomped foot in the air, and jumping about on the other one like a one-legged kangaroo. Georgette jumped up and down next to him, imitating him exactly, curses and all. She was perfect.

"Stop that! Stop that this instant! No more of your little pranks! Do you hear?"

She opened her eyes, and he could see her again. She stood very straight and saluted. "Yes, SIR," she shouted, her eyes ablaze with merriment.

"Now that you've had your little joke, my Pet, we'll get down to business. How do you propose to catch our little Princess, over there in the bower?"

"From this very spot, my Liege, I'll cast a spell on her."

"Yes, now you're talking. What kind of a spell?"

"I'll make her think she's cold and that our little cage has a woodstove and is warm and cozy like home, and that if she goes inside she can sit by the fire and toast her tootsies."

"It will never work."

"Why not?" she said, upset, her eyebrows raised, expectant, offended.

"You don't have the powers to cast such a spell."

"But I do, my Liege. I have been practicing and working and reading lots of books."

"Well, my Pet, if you can do it, go ahead. Give it a whirl."

"Okay, here goes." She crouched down and wiggled her fingers in the direction of Olivia, who was joking happily with Mr. Snake in the bower. She chanted the words of the spell with power and presence.

Charles F. D. Egbert

"Hocus-pocus, silver and gold,
You're really warm, but you think you're cold.
You should have done what your mother told,
And worn your sweater—however old.

"If you come here, as soon you'll see,
You'll be as warm as you'd like to be,
Until you come, you'll chatter and freeze,
But don't blame me, you can do as you please."

It was a good spell and properly done, and it worked, just like that.

"Here she comes," Georgette said, "hide!" She was gone in a jiffy, and big, fat, clumsy Count Carlos crouched, without a shred of dignity, behind a thorny raspberry bramble.

When Olivia came to the cart, she was shivering and one hand was clutching the collar of her thin cotton dress trying to keep her neck warm, and the other was holding Mr. Snake. She shuddered, and her teeth chattered from the strange cold.

"Heavens to Betsy! What's going on? I was having such a good talk with Mr. Snake and suddenly the air turned frigid. How can it be so cold? It's summertime! Mother was right! Why didn't I wear that old sweater? I wish I were in my room at home. I could sit by the fire and Mother would bring me a cup of tea. My fingers are like icicles." She stopped when she saw the cart. "What's that?" she asked, "and what's it doing here in the middle of the forest? Strange! It seems to be warmer over this way." The cart had a warm glow, and when she opened its gate she said, "Oh, yes, it's warm and toasty in here, just like home."

Mr. Snake was making such a fuss that she stopped and asked him what was the matter.

"Hissy-hissy-hissy-hiss."

"Oh, no, it'll be all right, you'll see," she said and, holding him under her arm, she foolishly got into the cart. "Oh, yes, this is much better. Yes, there's no place like home, there's no place like home."

As soon as she was in the cart, Count Carlos Maximillian von Dusseldorf leaped out from behind the raspberry bramble—WHOOSH, slammed the gate closed—BANG, and locked it—CLICK.

"We have her! Good work, my Pet. Your powers grow stronger every day." He hung the key on a nail at the end of the handle of the cart where Olivia couldn't reach.

"It is a pleasure to be of service, my Liege." Georgette's modesty was spectacular, and the way she batted her eyelids completely unaffected.

"Hey, what's going on?" Olivia cried out. The spell was over and she saw that she was trapped in a nasty, foul-smelling cage. "What am I doing here? I thought I was in the castle."

"That's what we wanted you to think, my Pretty." The Count giggled and rubbed his hands together. "You're ours now, my Pretty."

Olivia hated to be called stupid names like *my Pretty*. It was rude and presumptuous. Yes, of course, she was pretty, but the words coming from his foul mouth were vile and loathsome.

"I am not 'your Pretty,'" she said, stamping her foot. "Who are you anyway?"

"Allow me to introduce myself," he said with unrestrained arrogance as he strutted back and forth. "I am Count Carlos Maximillian von Dusseldorf the Fourth. My grandfather was the King of Portugal and a distinguished member of the House of Braganza. My grand-uncle-in-law was Maximillian the First, Holy Roman Emperor and bosom-buddy of Henry the Eighth. The vons were a noble Dutch family. I was born in a château in Dusseldorf."

"Have you finished?" Olivia was bored to tears.

"Listen, you pip-squeak, I've barely started."

"Count Carlos, did you say?"

"At your service, Madam." He made a great, big, sweeping, showy, stupid bow.

"And you are a gentleman?"

"Yes, of course." He was offended that she even felt the need to ask.

"Well, then, if you are a gentleman, and you are at my service, please get me out of this filthy cage at once."

The Count gave her a haughty smile and blinked his eyes in mock dismay. "My, my, we are forward aren't we?"

"I MEAN IT!" She glowered at him.

"All in good time, my Pretty."

"I AM NOT 'YOUR PRETTY'!"

"My goodness, but we have a sharp tongue, don't we?"

"You're not getting away with this. I'm going to tell my mother and father, and they're the King and the Queen around here, you know!"

"Yes, that's what I understand." He rubbed his hands together. "And I'm sure they would like to have you back, wouldn't they?"

"Yes, they would."

"Well, I'll see if that can be arranged."

"You mean, you're going to—do you mean that you're going to give me back to them?" She was baffled by this kind remark.

"Yes, of course, my Pretty—AS SOON AS I COLLECT THE RANSOM!" He sprayed the word RANSOM through the bars of the cage, right in her face.

"YOU CAN'T DO THIS TO ME," she shouted.

"What are you going to do, cry? Go ahead then, see if I care."

"NO, I'M NOT!" She wanted to, but this wasn't the time for tears.

Mr. Snake, at her side, was nodding not just his head but his whole body, because she was doing such a great job taking care of herself, something he wasn't very good at.

The Count slipped over to speak with Georgette, who was waiting for orders. "I can see that this is not going to be easy, and we don't have a lot of time. I've got to get going."

> *"Then we must hurry, you and me,*
> *Before the moon drinks up the sea."*

"What?" The Count hated verses. "Oh, never mind. Get your writing things, Georgette. I'll dictate the ransom note and take her to the swamp as soon as I've finished."

She got her chalk and a slate from the side of the cart where they were hanging between ratty long-underwear and a pair of broken suspenders. She sat down on a stone wall, arranging herself with the board in her lap and the chalk in her hand, ready for dictation.

"I am ready for dictation, Mr. Dictator," she said and smiled an impertinent smile.

The Count, frowning, paced back and forth in his most dictatorial manner, thinking.

"Now then," he started in, "how shall I address the King? Perhaps, 'Mr. Highness.'" Georgette wrote this on her board. "No, it's too simple." Georgette erased what she had written. "Maybe, 'Your Royal Loftiness.'" Georgette wrote. "No, it's too Alpine." Georgette erased. "Maybe something like, 'My Dear Fellow.'" She wrote. "No, no, it's too casual." She erased. "How about, 'Hey Horace.'" She rolled her eyes but didn't write—it was too stupid.

"What about, 'My Dear King'?" she suggested.

"Yes, that's just what I was going to say. Write it down. My Dear King," he went on. "Whereas, your lovely daughter is now in my possession . . ."

"I AM NOT AND I NEVER WILL BE." Olivia had been listening to him and was furious.

Mr. Snake hissed again to encourage her.

"And, whereas, if I feel like it, I will have her for lunch, she would be quite good stuffed and fricasseed and smothered with onions."

"I would not!"

"And, whereas, if you don't do as I tell you, she will get nothing to eat whatsoever."

"So what else is new?"

"And, whereas, since you are rich and I am poor . . ."

"We are not rich. Where did you ever get an idea like that?"

"Therefore, I demand that you give me all your money or a gazillion dollars, whichever is greater. Yours very truly and sincerely, I remain your obedient servant, Count Carlos M. von Dusseldorf. Dusseldorf, with two s's."

"Very good, my Liege," Georgette said, and finished writing with a charming flourish of the chalk.

"It will never work!" Olivia shook the bars of her cage.

"PS," said the Count, "Please do this as soon as possible because she's a big bother and talks too much."

As soon as Georgette wrote the PS, she sprang to her feet and skipped over to a nearby elm tree that had a handy nail sticking out of it.

> *"It now is written, I'll post it here.*
> *It's all spelled out and will cost them dear."*

She hung the ransom note on the tree and stood back to admire her work.

"Now then, my Pet, while I take her across the swamp, you

must make yourself invisible and wait here for them to come looking for her. It won't be long. Listen to them and tell me what they say."

> *"I'll watch what they say and hear what they do,*
> *And report the same day, the whole thing to you."*

"Would you just shut up with all that twaddle?"

"That's not twaddle," Olivia said, "It's poetry and it's quite nice actually."

"It is not."

"It is so."

"Who asked you?"

"Such an uncultured mind! You should be ashamed of yourself."

"Please, my Pet, put a little spell on that big mouth of hers, so that she doesn't irritate our fuzzy, furry, forest friends—and doesn't DRIVE ME CRAZY!"

"Don't you dare! I'll speak out against evil whenever it rears its ugly head!"

"Quickly, quickly, my Pet," he said, waving his arms, "before she says another word."

Georgette did a perfect cartwheel and landed delicately just in front of Olivia and wiggled her fingers as she cast the spell.

> *"Hocus-pocus, your tongue shall not speak,*
> *Out of focus, till sometime next week."*

"Thank you my Pet. What would I do without you?"

"It is my pleasure to do your bidding, my Liege." Her small, graceful bow was, in and of itself, an awesome work of art.

Olivia opened and closed her mouth several times but no sound came out. It was as if her vocal cords had taken a vacation to the Bahamas. It was very annoying. All she could do was shake her fist and wag her pointer-finger at them the way her mother did. Mr. Snake looked like he wanted to cry.

"I'm leaving now, Georgette. Make sure the King sees the ransom note, and then lead them to me in the forest. Don't forget." He picked up the handles of the cart and started to drag poor Olivia off into the darkness of the forest. "Man, this thing is really heavy."

"Serves you right!" was Olivia's comment—to herself, of course, because she couldn't talk. Georgette waved at them as they were leaving.

> *"Farewell, my Liege, I'll do my best,*
> *To watch these woods (or take a rest)."*

She said this with her little hands cupped daintily around her puckered mouth, her eyes twinkling with mischief, standing on her tippy-toes for emphasis, and whispering the *or take a rest* part so that the Count couldn't hear her.

"And none of your little pranks, my Pet," was the last thing the he shouted to her as he made his way into the forest.

> *"A prank or two or three or four,*
> *Is fun for you and me or more,*
> *But soon they'll come, I'll quiet be,*
> *And hide myself behind this tree."*

From the back of the cart, Olivia saw the sun setting behind the castle before the darkness of the forest closed in. In the other direction, she saw the Count's back as he trudged between the trees, with a swarm of blackflies around his head. How he knew where he was going was a mystery to her. He mumbled and stumbled and grumbled and fumbled and nearly tumbled, while she held on to the cart for dear life. Poor Mr. Snake seemed to be even more afraid than she was, and she held him tightly with one arm.

"This is the end," she said, "I'll never be able to help my mother and father now. I may never even see them again." She was sad and angry and shook the bars of her cage, but Count Carlos paid no attention.

Chapter Five

"Cora, my dear," the King said, rubbing his big toe, "shouldn't Olivia be back by now?" It was late afternoon and they were in the countinghouse with nothing to do.

"Oh, yes, gracious me." The Queen, always on the alert for trouble, had somehow forgotten the time. "Look," she said rushing to the window, "the sun is setting and she isn't back. SOMETHING HAS HAPPENED!" Panic struck a chord in her voice. "She's always here before the sun sets, that's the rule. Come, Horace, put your boots on and let's go."

This was typical of the Queen. When she had nothing else to do, she would nag and complain all day, but when an emergency appeared, she would swing into action like her father had when one of his cows was sick.

When they got to Olivia's bower, she wasn't there. They

peered into the forest and called to her, but their voices only echoed among the trees. "O-LIV-YA! O-liv-ya! . . . liv-ya! WHERE ARE YOU? Where are you? . . . are you?"

"Where could she be?" asked the Queen.

"I have no idea. She always plays right here," said the King.

"I knew it. I knew something like this would happen. I just knew it."

"We don't know what's happened yet. Maybe it's nothing."

"Nothing, indeed! Something terrible has happened—of course."

"Perhaps you are just worrying needlessly as you do about everything, ruining the peaceful, pleasant passage of time for everyone."

"I'm not worrying needlessly! I'm worrying purposefully."

"Whatever!"

Never, in all the time Olivia had gone to play in the bower, had she strayed or come back late, and now she was missing, and the sun was barely visible over the edge of the green hills, melting down like a glob of butter in a frying pan.

"Where could she be?" asked the Queen.

"I have no idea," replied the King.

"You don't think she would go out into the forest, do you?"

"No, I don't think so, but she might have."

"She was talking about picking some berries."

They put their arms around each other, and just as they were about to start crying, they heard someone singing.

"What's that?" said the King.

"Maybe—maybe it's a wild animal," said the Queen.

"It didn't sound like a wild animal. It sounded like some-one singing."

"Maybe it's a prehistoric monster who knows how to sing."

"Yes, I suppose that's a possibility."

Again, but much closer this time, came the voice. "Tra la la boom di ay. Tra la la boom di ay." It was a strong, deep voice.

"There it is again," shrieked the Queen, barely able to speak because she had stuffed all ten fingers into her mouth.

The King swung his cane about like a sword and shouted into the woods. "WHOEVER YOU ARE, COME OUT, SO THAT I CAN CUT OFF YOUR HEAD."

"Better wait, dear, and see who it is."

"We can see who it is later."

"Yes, dear, well, you know best."

"COME OUT NOW! I COMMAND YOU!" he said, using his most commanding voice.

The owner of this strong, deep voice appeared suddenly in the form of a handsome youth, as handsome as any young man in the Green Mountains. He was dressed in a uniform, brown shorts, a brown short-sleeved shirt, brown socks and shoes. He was very business-like and had a worried smile. On his shoulder he carried a brown leather bag full of letters and packages. He stopped when he saw the King and Queen.

"Excuse me, Your Highnesses," he said, having noticed their Royal Garments, "do you happen to know a party by the name of Princess Olivia? I have a letter for her."

"Who are you?" said the King.

"I am Prince Dropoffsky."

"Nice shorts," said the Queen, who liked casual attire.

"Thank you."

"You say that you're a Prince?"

"Yes, Sir. I come from the Ompompanoosuc River Valley, and when the snows melted this year, our beloved river flooded its banks and filled our land with oozing mud. My people have nothing to eat. They are impoverished."

"Where, exactly, is this river, whatever you call it?" asked the King. "I think I've heard of it. East of here, somewhere, isn't it?"

"North, actually."

Their long discussion about the location of the Ompompanoosuc River consumed valuable daylight and distracted them from the emergency at hand. The King asked about the

Prince's family, his heritage, and his estate. Meanwhile, their one and only daughter was being transported toward the Isthmus that divides the Long Swamp from the Short Swamp, over near Brandon.

"But why are you here?" asked the Queen.

"I have been cursed by a sorceress," the Prince explained, "to wander the paths and trails of the Kingdom until I find a long-lost maiden. When I have found her, I then have to hunt down Count Carlos Maximillian von Dusseldorf and put an end to his evil deeds. Only when I have done this will I be able to return to the Ompompanoosuc Valley and save my people." This lad was definitely noble and, except for being a bit pudgy, most attractive.

"Count Carlos?" asked the Queen, looking aghast.

"You know him?" The Prince was astounded that this reputable-looking lady should know someone as disreputable as the Count. "Personally?"

"Oh, no, I should say not! I know him only by reputation," she said, standing on her dignity.

"If I can put an end to the evil deeds of this Carlos person, I will save my people. This is my curse. It is written and I will obey. And when I've done it, I won't have to wear these ridiculous shorts anymore."

"I like them." The Queen had taken a fancy to this young man.

"Thank you."

"Did you say, young man, that you are looking for a Long-Lost Maiden?" asked the King.

"Yes, I am."

"How long lost?"

"Oh, very long. Very long lost."

"Well, maybe we can help you."

"Really? Do you know any long-lost maidens?"

"Yes, we do. Our daughter."

"How long has she been lost?"

"Well, actually, now that you mention it, not all that . . ."

"A long time," said the Queen, pushing the King aside, "a very long time." This wasn't the place to quibble about the passage of time, and, at least to her, it already seemed like her own sweet Olivia had been gone for decades, simply decades, instead of perhaps an hour.

"I see," said the Prince, suddenly very interested. "What's her name?"

"Olivia," the Royal Couple said together proudly.

"Olivia? Olivia? That sounds familiar." He plunged himself into thought.

"She's very nice," said the Queen.

"She's a real Princess," said the King.

"But sometimes she doesn't act like a Princess."

"But we love her anyway."

"Aha!" said the Prince, "That's the name on my letter." He reached into his bag and pulled out an envelope with her name written on it in formal script. "Yes, that's the name, it's right here on this envelope. So if I can find her and give her this, I can kill two birds with one stone." He put the letter carefully back into his bag.

"WHAT?" The Queen squealed like a stuck pig. "YOU KILL BIRDS WITH STONES?"

"Oh, no, Your Highness, that's just an expression I use. I wouldn't dream of doing anything like that. I come from a long line of bleeding-heart pacifists. It's in the blood around here."

"Yes, so do we," said the King, trying to patch things up.

"Then you don't kill birds with stones?" she asked plaintively.

"Why no, of course not, I wouldn't dream of doing such a thing?"

"I see. Well, then, I guess it's all right. I'm sorry."

"No harm done," the Prince said magnanimously. "Now then, back to business. Where did you lose this daughter?"

"Oh, we didn't lose her."

"But I thought you said . . ."

"She lost herself."

"Why did you say that?" the King asked the Queen.

"Well, I didn't want him to think it was our fault."

"She lost herself? How could she do that? Where did you last see her?"

"She was playing right here in the bower this very afternoon, and now, as you can see, she's not here."

"Maybe she wandered off. Maybe she's playing hide-and-seek."

"By herself?"

"Yes, it comes naturally to lonely children."

"Really!" They were impressed with his knowledge of child psychology.

"Aha!" said the Prince. "I know! I know exactly what has happened. Yes! Indubitably! She has been captured by Count Carlos Maximillian von Dusseldorf, my archenemy and my nemesis."

"We don't know that for a fact," said the King, "we just know that she's not here."

"I will help you find her." The Prince was a noble fellow indeed and also courteous, kind, obedient, cheerful, thrifty, brave, clean, and reverent. "I assure you that I will find her."

"How can you be so sure?" said the Queen.

"It just so happens that I have the nose of a bloodhound."

"You do?" said the King, who was more literal-minded than the Queen. "You don't look like you have the nose of a bloodhound."

The Queen poked him in the ribs. "He just means that he smells good."

"Really?" The King knew lots of people who smelled bad, even from a distance, but very few who smelled good, and he was curious. So with his hands in his pockets, whistling an airy tune, he ambled over to the noble but unsuspecting Prince and, without being noticed, took a good sniff. When he was quite finished, he went back to the Queen and whispered in her ear, "So he does, so he does," and she gave him another sharp poke in the ribs for being so stupid.

"What?" he said. He didn't like to get poked in the ribs, particularly when he had done nothing wrong.

"Now then, to work." The Prince threw himself down on his hands and knees and started sniffing around among the ferns, his nose twitching like an old bloodhound. Suddenly he stopped and pointed to a place where Olivia had been sitting a few hours before. He pointed to the spot, not with his nose like a real bloodhound, but with his pointer-finger.

"Aha!" he shouted. "She was here. Right here."

"We know where she was. What we don't know is where she is."

The Prince again put his handsome aquiline nose to the ground and sniffed around in ever-expanding circles. Soon he was able to smell the nasty feet of the evil Count.

"Aha!" he shouted again. *Aha!* was one of his favorite expressions and was very useful when searching for long-lost maidens. "Count Carlos was there. Right there," he said, pointing again. "Pwewf." A real bloodhound wouldn't have expressed himself in a manner quite so prejudicial.

"Can you smell his tracks? Which way do they lead?" said the Queen.

"This way! Come, we'll follow them."

"You lead the way, and we'll bring up the rear," said the King.

By this time it was quite dark and they could barely see where they were going. The King, with Royal Grandeur, Pomp, and Circumstance, reached into the Royal Pocket of his Royal Breeches and produced two streamlined, semi-automatic, air-cooled, hand-operated flashlights, and said, "This one is for you, my darling."

"You remembered to bring flashlights?" She couldn't believe

that old Horace, who, on occasion, forgot his name, and, from time to time, one shoe, could have thought of bringing flashlights. "Thank you, my dear."

"Yes, of course. Don't I always provide what is necessary?"

The short answer would have been no, but she had turned to the Prince. "Do you have one of these, Prince Dropoffsky?"

"Of course! Be prepared, is what I say."

"Why do you say that? Are you a Boy Scout?"

"As a matter of fact, I am."

"Can you build a fire and do you have lots of merit badges?"

"I can and I do."

"Would you stop pestering the man with all these unnecessary questions so that we can get going?"

"I was just being polite." For the Queen, politeness came before practically everything.

The Prince threw his bag over his shoulder. "This way," he said and led them out of the bower into the forest. It was dark and their flashlights flashed hither and thither onto the trees and leaves, making furious shadows, and the squirrels, muskrats, porcupines, deer, and even the bears and moose wondered what on earth was going on.

The Royal Couple were extremely grateful that this gracious young Prince had come along. He was just in time to help them and would now—or if not now, soon—lead them to their cherished daughter, their one-and-only Olivia.

They made their way to the place where the Count's cart had stood. They could see the tracks made by the cart wheels in the dirt and follow them through the underbrush.

"Now it will be easy," said the Prince.

What they couldn't see, because she had her eyes closed, was the wondrous, wily, winsome Georgette, focusing her fanciful fingers at the ransom note she had hung on a tree. She hadn't expected them to come at night, so, at the last minute she had conjured up a light so they could see the sign.

"Aha! The ransom note!" said the Prince, "Just as I suspected!"

Chapter Six

While the Royal Couple and Prince Dropoffsky were reading the ransom note, Count Carlos was pulling Princess Olivia in his cart across the covered bridge toward Woodchuck Hill and past that to Sunset Lake. In this part of the Green Mountains, the trees were so gigantic that it would take four or five people holding hands to give one of them a hug, and had huge branches and leaves that practically touched the sky.

Count Carlos groped his way through the forest by the light of the silvery moon, and finally, when he couldn't go on any longer, he found a clearing that had room enough to put the cart and build a fire. Above his head, through a small, pocket-handkerchief-sized opening in the canopy, a few friendly moonbeams did their best to penetrate the darkness. He wiped his brow and stopped.

"Whew, I'm tired. That stupid cart must weigh a ton, probably two tons with you in it."

Olivia paid no attention to this insult and waited while he collected twigs and branches to build a fire. She liked the smell of the smoke, and watched the flames flicker and send wild and glorious shadows into the trees. She squinted at him when he had the fire going, half because of the smoke that was coming her way and half because he was such an awful person.

During the journey through the forest, she had been frightened and sad. Mr. Snake, who was usually cheery and pleasant, had very little to hiss about except to advise her to keep a stiff upper lip, which was kind of him, but didn't really help much.

Olivia couldn't speak because of the spell that Georgette had put on her that was supposed to last "until sometime next week." Well, it didn't! It lasted only a couple of hours, and by the time they got there, she had saved up a lot of things to say to the Count, mostly advice on how to improve himself and be a better person. So when he said, "Whew, I'm really tired!" for about the tenth time, she had forgotten about the spell and spoke up.

"That's because you're not in good condition. You wouldn't be so tired if you took better care of yourself."

"WHAT?" He was astounded that she would say such a thing about him and also that she could say anything at all.

"You're lazy and overweight, you don't get enough exercise, and you don't eat your vegetables." She didn't actually know about his vegetables but said it with authority and sounded like her mother.

"I am not, and I do too, and besides you can't talk!"

"I can so. What do you think I'm doing?"

"You can't! Georgette put a spell on you and you can't say a word."

"It wore off."

"Impossible!"

"It is not!"

"It is so! And besides I don't need any advice from you, you're just a child and not a very bright one at that."

This last comment showed the depth of Count Carlos's stupidity. Anyone, even the most ludicrous, lazy lout could see that she was not just bright but very bright, able to do anything she set her mind to. She could learn anything, play any game, climb any mountain, and sing any song—if only she could get out of that nasty cage.

"I am so!" Olivia shot back.

"You am so what?"

"Bright!"

"You am not."

"Yes, I am."

This argument went back and forth for some time before Count Carlos remembered the old arithmetic trick. "Okay, if you're so smart, how much is 1,234 divided by 5,678? Huh? Huh? Huh?"

"I don't know!" Olivia tossed her proud head. "It's a stupid question. No one can do long division without pencil and paper."

"So you see, that proves it."

"Proves what?

"That you aren't as smart as you think you are."

"Well, I can't do long division in my head, but I know how to be a nice person, and that's more than you know."

"What does a little twit of a girl know about anything? What can you tell me that I don't already know?"

"Plenty!"

"Well, why don't you tell me everything you know. Let's see, that should take about ten seconds," he said, sneering at her and folding his arms on top of his big belly.

"You need to learn how to be nice."

"Oh, here we go."

"Being nice is not very hard."

"Izzat right?"

"You have to be pleasant to people and smile at them when you see them at a church supper or on the village green."

"Smile?" he said incredulously. "Smile? Why should I smile? What good does it do? Smiling is for sissies."

"You should smile so that people know that you are a nice person."

"What a bunch of blither-blather."

"You can't do it, can you?"

"What do you mean! Of course I can! Everyone can smile."

"Well, go ahead then. Let's see you do it."

Count Carlos stopped poking his stick into the fire and tried to smile. Now, this was really something to see. The grunting and heaving and stressing and straining! I've never seen a man pick up a cow, but that's what he looked like. And not only that, but it hurt! His face was so twisted and contorted that even his mother wouldn't have recognized him.

"Call that a smile?" she jeered at him from the cage. "I mean a real smile—from the heart—like this." And she smiled a sweet, soft, simple smile.

Count Carlos was amazed for a moment, but then he was disgusted with himself for being awed by a little girl's smile. "Oh, give me a break!" he said and went back to poking the fire.

"Well, that's how it's done, but it takes practice, you can't expect to do it the first time you try."

"I could do it if I wanted to, but I don't want to. So there!" he said and pouted.

The Count was second to none when it came to pouting. His dark eyes and fat, protruding lower lip were perfectly suited to this endeavor. But a little pouting didn't stop Olivia—she was still talking, giving advice.

"It's not very hard. You have to listen to people even if you don't like what they say."

"Balderdash!"

"And think of others especially if they're not feeling well."

"Nonsense!"

"Nice people keep themselves clean and tidy."

"I prefer to be dirty and messy."

"And help their mother and father every day."

"Mother and father? Are you kidding? My mother and father have been locked up since before I was born."

"Really? That's dreadful!" She looked at him sympathetically, trying to show him, by example, what a nice person would do.

"And they deserved it. They were a couple of mugs if I ever saw one."

"Mugs?" Olivia chirped, having never heard the word used that way.

"Yeah, that's what I said—mugs. You know, deadbeats, yazoos, schlemiels, thugs, brainless wonders, whacker-knickers, meatballs . . ."

"What did they do that was so bad?" she asked pleasantly, although it was a distasteful subject.

"DO?" he shouted, and the thunder of his voice ricocheted among the trees, causing a murmur among our fuzzy, furry, forest friends, some of whom had awakened from sweet hopeful dreams about being friends with human beings once again.

"Yes, what did they do?" she asked again, consistently, maddeningly pleasant.

"DO? DO?" he shouted again and started counting on his fingers. "I'll tell you what they did: They smuggled, loitered, smoked, cheated, stole, embezzled, and there was tax evasion, fraud, mayhem, and lying about their age." That was ten and he ran out of fingers and was about to take his boots off so he could count on his toes.

"No, no, that's all right, I get the idea." Olivia was concerned about the terrible odor that might come from his boots, not for herself, of course, but for the forest and all of its dear creatures.

"But why did they do those things?" She was concerned.

"Because they were nutso, crazy, bonkers, and stupid, some of their pages were stuck together, they were looney-tunes, not the brightest bulbs in the marquee, and half a sandwich short of a picnic, that's why."

"But can't you see, they were that way because they were not nice, not nice to each other, or to anybody else. Being nice is very important."

"You sound like a broken record, and besides, who cares about that sort of fussy stuff?"

"Everyone who has any self-respect."

"People like you, I suppose, and look where it got you— locked up inside a small cage with a big lock."

"And it wouldn't hurt if you took a bath once a year, whether you needed it or not."

"I tried that once. Didn't like it."

"You are smelly, disgusting, stupid, and uncouth."

"If you're so smart and I'm so stupid, why are you on the inside of that cage and I'm on the outside?"

"Cleaning your fingernails would be nice, and a haircut and shampoo now and then wouldn't be a bad idea either."

"Ah, shuddup, would you? I've had enough of your nitter-nattering." He got up from the fire, collected some pine needles, and made a pile to sleep on.

"Don't put them too close to the fire."

"DON'T TELL ME WHERE TO PUT MY PINE NEEDLES!"

"Well, go ahead then, put them right in the fire if you want to. See if I care."

The Count put his pine needles in a heap (at a safe distance from the fire) and made an indentation in the middle, like I do with my mashed potatoes to make a place to put the gravy, only in this case, he, the Count himself, was the gravy. When it was ready, he poured himself in and wiggled around until he was comfortable.

"I'm cold," Olivia whimpered.

"So what?"

He was snoring before she could say Jack Robinson.

"I'm sorry, Mr. Snake, it's all my fault."

"Hissy-hissy."

"Oh, well, it's nice of you to say that, but I really don't know what to do. Do you think my mother and father will ever notice that I'm missing?"

"Hissy-hissy."

"Well, I hope so."

She heard the mournful howl of a coyote and shivered with the cold. Then her throat got tight, and her chin quivered, and her mouth turned down at both corners, and suddenly she was crying. She hadn't meant to—she had meant to be brave and was very disappointed with herself, but crying felt so good that she just cried and didn't think about whether she was supposed to or not.

"Will they ever come to find me? If they don't come and get me out of this cage, how will I ever be able to help them?"

Chapter Seven

"**W**hat's that?" cried the Queen.

"It's a Ransom Note," said the Prince.

"What does it say?" asked the King, who hadn't brought his glasses.

"It says: 'My Dear King. Whereas, blah, blah, blah, blah, blah, blah, blah, blah, therefore, you must pay me a gazillion dollars.' Signed, Count Carlos M. von Dusseldorf. Dusseldorf with two *s*'s."

"Oh me, oh my, that's just what I was afraid of," said the Queen.

"It's him, then. What shall we do?" said the King.

"We'll follow him to the edge of the earth and push him off, or, if that doesn't work, we'll find out what he eats and starve him to death." The Royal Couple were pleased that the Prince was making these helpful, rational decisions and approved the second plan.

"Follow me," he said confidently and strode off into the forest. The King and Queen scurried after him, struggling to keep up. The Prince stopped from time to time, getting down on his hands and knees to sniff the ground and check for Count Carlos's footprints. For the most part, he was able to see the trail that was made by the wheels of the cart because the ground was soft and the tracks were fresh. He stopped under a spreading oak tree to check his map, and the Royal Couple pointed their lights to the place where his pointer-finger touched the map.

"He's headed directly toward the Large Swamp," he said, "and will, without doubt, cross Seager Hollow Road, and then go past Hawk Hill and that's where we'll find him. We'll have to walk all night so we can catch up."

"Walk all night!" said the King, who had been hoping that the Prince would suggest that they stop and sleep, and set out again in the morning when it was light and they weren't so tired. "All night?"

"Oh, Horace, do try to be brave."

"I am trying." But he wasn't succeeding. He didn't feel brave. His toe hurt and he wanted to go home.

"Think of it as an adventure, dear, you've always liked adventure."

"I don't like adventure. Whatever gave you that idea?"

"That's what you say when you're bored."

"I do not."

"Yes, you do. You say that you wish you had more adventure in your life."

"I don't always say that—just once in a while—when I feel like it."

"Which is most of the time." She patted him on the head hoping to cheer him up, but it only irritated him.

They continued walking through the forest, down a hill, through a glade, over a stream, and, although they were nowhere near Olivia, the Queen decided it would be a good idea to call to her just in case. "Olivia?" she cried out tentatively, into the night, hoping to hear Olivia's sweet voice call back, "I'm over here, Mother," and all this insane roaming around in the middle of the night would be over.

"Be quiet!" said the Prince sharply. "You mustn't give away our position."

"He's right, Cora, we mustn't give away our position. It's one of the rules." The King had studied the rules of warfare many years ago and had forgotten most of them, and the Queen didn't even know what they meant by *position*, but they were men and supposedly understood this sort of military terminology.

They came to a large, flat face of rock. It was as big as a house and completely devoid of trees, ferns, or even dirt. After a few steps across the ledge, the good Prince could no longer follow the trail.

"I have lost the scent," he whispered to them. "Wait here. I'll try to find where Count Carlos went back into the forest." He walked slowly around the edge of the rock face, sniffing carefully and flashing his light back and forth, leaving the King and Queen to fend for themselves, but fending was not what they wanted to do right then, so they stood close together, frightened, and looked over each other's shoulders into the darkness.

The Prince returned after he had explored the circumference of Rock Face without finding any trace of the cart tracks going back into the forest. "The trail is lost!" he said.

"Lost?" said the Queen.

"I can find no traces, no tracks, no scents—nothing! I'm at a complete loss." He was a sad sight with his eyes downcast, defeated in his efforts to find Princess Olivia.

"Perhaps the Count didn't go across the ledge at all," said the King.

"Don't be absurd, Horace, he had to. If he went in, he had to come out."

"Not necessarily." The King was not to be dismissed easily.

"Don't be ridiculous, Horace."

"Maybe—maybe he came out the same way he went in."

"Why would he do that? What good is it to go in and then come out in the same place? How would he ever get anywhere?"

He hadn't thought of that.

"Aha!" shouted Prince Dropoffsky, his eyes gleaming with insight. "The Old Double-Back Trick!" He dropped to his knees and, with the help of the flashlights held by the King and Queen, looked again at the tracks that led into the Rock Face.

"Look!" he shouted and sprang up, almost knocking the Royal Couple onto their Royal Behinds. He pointed down at the ground. "Double tracks! Right there! Clear as a bell! So the tricky old buzzard tried to fool me, but I'm too smart for him."

"But, Prince Dropoffsky, it was *my* idea." The King seldom had a good idea, but when he did, he wanted credit for it. His comment, however, was lost on the Prince as he headed back in the direction that they had come.

They retraced their steps for less than twenty feet before Prince Dropoffsky noticed several burr bushes that were bent over and a set of tracks that veered off in between some birch trees that were bending this way and that.

"Aha!" he proclaimed predictably. "Just as I thought." He was doing a good job especially considering that it was night. "This way," he said, and pushed his way through the underbrush closely following the tracks with his flashlight.

The moon was at its zenith when they arrived at a place where the ground was soft and soggy, and then, a little farther along, they found a large mud puddle. From footprints all about, and branches cut from pine trees, the Prince deduced that the cart had been stuck and that Count Carlos had struggled mightily to pull and pry it out of the muck.

"Excellent!" said the Prince. "This has made him lose time. He can't be far away now." He didn't know that Count Carlos was sound asleep next to a very smoky fire, miles from there.

Then the Prince said, "Wait a minute," and stopped in his tracks.

"What is it?" the Royal Couple said together.

"I heard something." Fear poured over them like freezing rain, dampening their spirits, and they stood as still as snowmen, listening. But all they heard were a few frogs who were quitting for the night, packing up their instruments and getting ready to go home.

"I thought I heard a noise," said the Prince.

"A swamp noise?"

"Perhaps."

"Are we near the swamp?"

"I don't know."

"I don't like it out here anymore," said the King, "I think I'll go home. I'm bored with this."

"You can't go home, Horace, it's too far and you'll get lost."

"I can't go on. My toe hurts and I can't walk anymore."

"Prince Dropoffsky," said the Queen, "why don't we sit for a while. The King needs a rest."

"Good thinking! We'll rest here for three minutes and then march on so that we can catch the Count with his pants down."

"Oh, deary me," said the Queen, "I hope not."

"Oh, no, I didn't mean it that way. I meant that we'll surprise him. It's just a figure of speech."

"Oh, well, in that case, I guess it's all right."

So they sat on the forest floor and rested except that it wasn't very restful. The Prince had heard a noise, so now, of course, they all did—loons, bats, hawks, foxes, even nightingales, and those underground creatures like moles that go rhrhrh, and ekekek, and chakchakchak, all making so much noise that they got no rest at all.

Without them knowing it, Georgette was watching from nearby and decided that this was a great opportunity for a few merry pranks! "Hoot, hoot, hoo-hoo," she cried out, standing at arm's length from the Queen, who, completely terrified, flung herself into the unsuspecting arms of the King who was sitting on a stump with his eyes closed and the right Royal Boot removed, massaging his big toe. She knocked him

over backward, and they went sprawling into a clump of ferns that, until that very moment, had been minding their own business. They shouted wildly for help, both thinking that a wild beast had attacked them. The Prince, who had been peering into the forest in the opposite direction, turned and saw what looked like a monster with two heads, four arms, and four legs. He prepared to defend himself. Why, he wondered, was it screaming for help with two voices. When they picked themselves up and put their crowns back on their heads, he realized that it was the King and the Queen, and said, casually, "Oh, it's you."

"Well, who did you think it was?" said the Queen in a huff, smoothing out the wrinkles in her skirt and trying to regain a smidgen of personal dignity while the King was poking around in the ferns for his flashlight.

This small crisis caused a great commotion in the lives of our furry, fuzzy, forest friends, and a great communal wail rose up, washing whispers and murmuring echoes back and forth through the woods. It came from a thousand voices large and small, speaking in all kinds of animal languages, saying, in one way or another, "Hey, pipe down out there, we're trying to sleep." This wail grew to a crescendo and frightened the Royal Couple and the Prince as well, but he had dealt with this sort of thing before, and, in order to bolster his courage as well as theirs, he sang a little song that went like this:

> *"There's nothing to fear, there's nothing to fear,*
> *We're out here having a lark.*
> *There's nothing to fear, there's nothing to fear,*
> *We'll whistle out here in the dark."*

Then he whistled "Yankee Doodle," and although it was seriously off-key and out of tune, it helped.

Georgette, to complicate the situation, roared like a lion and sent them all into a very friendly but undignified hug, but the Prince sang his little song again, and they all whistled and when they had finished, the Prince said, "Let's get out of here. This place gives me the creeps."

"Not only that but it stinks," said the King.

"You can say that again," said the Queen.

"Not only that but it stinks," said the King.

They set off again just in the nick of time, because Georgette was sucking in a great quantity of air preparing to make a terrible, thunderous, crumbling sound, something between the breakup of the ice in spring and the crashing down of a giant oak in a thunderstorm.

Chapter Eight

While Count Carlos was curled up on top of his pile of pine needles, warmed by the fire, Olivia shivered in his nasty, foul-smelling cage.

"Mumble, mumble, mumble," he mumbled, half asleep, and then, "mumble, mumble," followed by a comment she couldn't quite hear about pizza. This was followed by a great smacking of fat lips, salivating, and general groans and murmurs.

Being a very resourceful girl, she immediately saw possibilities in these mumbles, something she could use.

She started out very quietly. "Yes, pizza. Nice, warm, gooey pizza, with tomatoes and cheese and anchovies. Oh, yes."

"Mmm. Anchovies," he said without waking up.

"And mushrooms and pepperoni and cheese and sausage."

"Mmm. Sausage."

"And cheese and sausage and pepperoni and mushrooms."

"Mmm, mmm, mmmushrooms."

He rolled over on his back and his mouth watered until it was full, and each time he said, "Mmm," it sounded like he was gargling, "Mmmblugablugabluga. Mmmblugablugabluga."

"All you have to do to get this warm, mouthwatering pizza, is to . . ." Her voice was soft and soothing.

"Yes? Yes?" Although the Count was asleep, he understood everything she said. He pushed his head up into the air like a turtle on its back, straining his neck muscles.

"All you have to do to get some of this pizza . . ."

He got to his feet. "Yes?"

"Come closer and I'll tell you."

With his eyes closed and still sound asleep, he walked over to the cart, his hands out in front of him. "Yes. What do I have to do?"

"All you have to do is . . ."

"Yes? Yes? What?"

"Get the key . . ."

"Key? No, no, no, I don't think I'd better do that."

She had to be careful: She didn't want him to wake up. She continued in an even lower voice, emphasizing the adjectives. "Juicy chunks of spicy sausage and heavenly, melted cheese."

Slowly, Count Carlos took the key off the nail and started to put it into his mouth.

"No, not yet, not until you have put it into the padlock and turned it, then you can eat."

Again, the Count hesitated, his body trembling with conflict and anticipation.

"You'll have some pizza as soon as you turn the key."

The Count was so close that she could have snatched the key from his hand, but she didn't dare, because she knew that he would wake up and not let her escape.

"No. I don't think I should do that."

"No pizza if you don't. None for you."

"All right, all right," he whimpered. He turned the key so slowly that Olivia thought she was going to faint. Her heart pounded and she was standing with her knees bent and Mr. Snake in one hand, poised like a sprinter just before the starting gun is fired, ready to dash for safety. She could see beads of perspiration on the top of his bald head as he turned the key.

Finally, she heard a little *click* as the padlock released its steel jaws, and then he slowly pulled it out of the hasp and the door began to open.

"No, no, I don't think so," he said as he started to close the door again.

"Free garlic bread," she whispered in his ear, and she could see the rest of his resistance sag and crumble and he slowly opened the door.

Unfortunately, the hinges on the door were rusty and made a sharp squeak that woke him up.

"OH, NO YOU DON'T," he said, slamming the door in her face. "I'M NOT FALLING FOR THAT STUPID PIZZA TRICK. I WASN'T BORN YESTERDAY YOU KNOW."

Olivia was disappointed but refused to let on. "If you don't want any, that's fine. I don't care. I'm not hungry!"

"HA! WHAT A MORON! LITTLE SNIP OF A THING! OUTRAGEOUS! TOOK ME FOR A SIMPLE-TON DIDN'T YOU? THOUGHT YOU COULD FOOL ME DID YOU? WELL, YOU'VE GOT ANOTHER THINK COMING. ALL THIS TALK ABOUT PIZZA! WHAT A JOKE! WHAT? FOOL AN OLD HAND LIKE ME? HA! NEVER!" He put the key back on its nail and humphed around for a while, muttering about how stupid she was, and what did she think she was doing, repeating the same things over and over. After a while, fatigue got the best of him; he settled down again and went back to sleeping and snoring.

"It's not polite to snore," she said, but he snored even louder to show her that he didn't care what she thought.

When he was asleep and the forest was quiet again, she felt horribly alone and bit her lip so that she wouldn't cry. It worked for a while but then her lip started to hurt, so she let her lip go and started to cry. Crying was good and she let out all her bad feelings about the terrible situation she was in and her frustration that no one was coming to rescue her.

The key, hanging on its nail at the end of the handle of the cart, was only an inch or two farther than she could reach. Maybe she could get it if she had something to snag it with—a short piece of wire or even a pencil would do. She looked around and saw a twig on the ground that might work if she could get it. It wasn't far from the cart, but no matter how she tried, even lying on her stomach in the cart, she couldn't reach it, so she reached through the bars at the back of the cage for one of old Grouchface's saucepans. She was able to pull the saucepan from its hook without any trouble, but it was too big to fit between the bars of the cage so she passed it from hand to hand all the way around to the front of the cart. The only light she had came from the embers of the Count's dying campfire and an occasional moonbeam. She worked quietly. She held the saucepan by the edge so she could use the handle to hook the key. She was concentrating with all her might.

"Hi," came a voice out of nowhere.

She jumped and dropped the saucepan, and there was Georgette, resplendent, gorgeous, smiling radiantly at her.

"Oh, hello. You frightened me."

"Look at that," said Georgette, pointing to the Count. "Sleeping on the job. What would he do without me?"

"How are you?" Princess Olivia hoped that Georgette would help her.

"Fine, thank you, and I have news for you."

"News? Really? What sort of news?"

"Your hero is coming to save you."

"I don't have a hero."

"You do now."

"I do? What's he like?"

"He's cute—too old for you, but cute."

"Really? How exciting!"

"And he's coming with your mom and dad, His and Her Majesties."

"To rescue me?"

"Well, that's what they say, but, judging from what they do, I'm not sure."

"I can't wait."

"If your father gives my master a gazillion dollars, you can go free."

"But my father doesn't have a gazillion dollars."

"My Liege here, sound asleep, seems to think he does."

"How would he know?"

"He knows everything."

"And you have to do whatever he says?"

"Yes, at least when he's around. Otherwise, I do what I want."

"Why don't you run away?"

"Because I can't."

"Why not?"

"Well, you see, I used to be a bronze statue, and I sat on a shelf for years, simply years, until . . ."

"Until what?"

"Well, one day old Greedy-Grumpy here wandered into the shop looking for a bargain. When he saw me he stopped in his tracks and stared at me for about an hour without blinking. When you are as beautiful as I am, this happens quite frequently." She said this without a trace of vanity. "He looked so hard I felt like blushing, but of course I couldn't. Finally, he looked down at my price tag, said, 'Too much,' and walked out."

"Did he come back the next day?"

"No, he came back that night. I heard him pick the lock and then open the door. He came over to me, looked me in the eye, and told me that he would release me from being a bronze statue and would return me to my former self, if I would be his minion for ninety-nine years and do whatever he wanted, no matter how awful. I agreed immediately, of course. He made me swear a special oath, which I did gladly, and then he put this little hat on my head—this one, the one I'm wearing—and, ZAPPO! I was alive, and glad to be flesh and blood, breathing, and all the rest."

"That's a wonderful story, but where did he get the hat in the first place?"

"The King of the Mountain gave it to him during the blizzard of 'eighty-eight on the Feast of Steven—'and all the snow lay 'round about, cold and crisp and even.'"

"Really! How poetical."

Georgette told her one story after another until they realized that the sun was up.

"I didn't know you were so nice," Olivia told her.

"I'm not. I'm just pretending."

The Count woke with a snort, yawned, and scratched his head. When he saw Georgette, he struggled to his feet.

"Ah, you're back, my Pet! What news? What news abroad?"

"The King and Queen are on their way, with a charming young Prince."

"In shining armor?"

"No, in brown shorts."

"Oh, that Prince. I know him. He's a bother. The next time you see him, change him into newt or a hedgehog or something for two or three hundred years. Teach him a lesson."

Georgette struck a charming pose.

> *"The frog shall be gone,*
> *Ere morn doth come,*
> *And all small creatures,*
> *Lie down and play dumb."*

"Whatever that means!"

"That was very nice," said Olivia and clapped her hands and then frowned at the Count. "It's not nice to make fun of someone's poetry."

"There she goes again! Please, my Pet, cast a spell on that big mouth of hers, it's forever going on and on giving advice. I hate advice, and there's nothing I hate worse than *good* advice."

"I will give praise wherever praise is due."

"Quickly, quickly, my Pet, and do it properly. Your last spell didn't last."

"Yes, Sir."

Georgette turned to Olivia.

> *"Do what you will, do what you may,*
> *But no more voice will you have today."*

Princess Olivia opened her mouth but nothing happened; she couldn't make a peep. It was like when she was learning to whistle but could only blow air. She shook her fist at the Count and stamped her foot. She was also angry at Georgette whom she had thought was her friend.

"Ah, yes, much better, my Pet. Now we can enjoy the quiet." The Count sighed and eased himself into the vast, luxurious, embrace of the silence of the forest as if it were a warm bath—except, of course, that the Count, if we take him at his word, didn't like baths, warm or otherwise.

When he wasn't looking, Georgette whispered to Olivia,

> *"I'm sorry, my friend, if you can't sing a song,*
> *But soon 'twill be over, it won't last for long."*

"Come here, my little one," said the Count, "and tell me what you have seen."

Georgette explained.

> *"The Queen is quite near,*
> *Her voice is real clear,*
> *But she'd rather be eating pie.*
> *The King has come,*
> *His will to be done,*
> *But he sounds like he's ready to cry.*
> *The Prince, who just led them,*
> *Through bog and through bedlam,*
> *Is a hero, a wonderful guy."*

"But where are they, my Pet?"

"They are coming, my Liege."

"When, my Pet?"

"Now, my Liege."

Just at that moment, as though to prove her point, they heard the Royal Search Party shouting, "Olivia! Olivia!"

The Count went to peer into the forest toward the voices he had heard, and Georgette whispered to Olivia.

PRINCESS OLIVIA

"The Count can't count,
But don't count him out.
He'll think of something sly."

"Quickly, my Pet, quickly. They're coming. I'll pull the cart out of sight so that when they come to fetch their dear little Princess, I can jump out and grab them and fleece them for all they're worth." He pulled the cart behind some trees and hid nearby, waiting like a mousetrap set to go off when the cage door opened.

Chapter **Nine**

The members of the Royal Search Party, who had been walking all night, were exhausted and were now only a few hundred steps from their goal.

The Prince stopped suddenly and held his hands out to stop the King and Queen as if they were about to step into a mud puddle. "Aha! Just as I suspected. Smoke! I smell smoke."

"Smoke?"

"Really?"

"Yes. Indubitably! This way! Shhh!" And he led them toward the Count's campfire, sneaking through the forest like a cat stalking a mouse. The King and Queen, seeing him do this, decided that if he did it, it must be important, so they began sneaking through the forest like cats stalking mice as well, which was all very well for the Queen but caused the King a good deal of pain because of his bad toe.

They peered through the leaves at the campfire. No one was there. Slowly, they came into the clearing and stood around the fire to warm their hands and "tootsies," as Georgette liked to say. If they had looked more carefully into the forest, they would have seen Olivia in the moonlight, locked in a cart, speechless and waving to them like a flag on the Fourth of July.

"I know that this is Count Carlos's campfire. He can't be far away."

"We've been searching all night. Where could she be?" said the Queen.

"The tracks led to this very spot," said the Prince.

"We've looked behind every rock and under every tree," said the King.

"We cannot give up now. We must find her. We mustn't lose heart."

"The Prince says that we mustn't lose heart, dear," said the King.

"I'm not losing my heart—I'm losing my mind," said the Queen.

"Well," said the King, trying to be supportive, "that's not so bad, I suppose."

"What we need is a sign," said the Prince. "Something that will tell us what to do next." The Royal Couple heartily agreed and they all listened for a moment hopefully. Unfortunately, the forest, as is usually the case, offered nothing at all in the way of signs.

"Why doesn't she call out?" said the Queen.

"Or do something?" replied the King.

"Yes, so I could tell her not to."

The Prince was distraught that the Count was not where he was supposed to be. "All I ask for is a simple clue."

And the Queen agreed. "Yes, a little something to help us."

"Because we're so tired," added the King.

At this point, Mr. Snake got Princess Olivia's attention and hissy-hissed in her ear.

"Oh," she said, forming the words carefully so that he could read her lips. "That's a great idea! Are you sure?"

"Hissy-hiss."

"All right. Here goes." She slipped the very brave Mr. Snake out between the bars of her cage, aimed carefully, and threw him between the trees where he landed at the Prince's feet.

The Prince picked him up. "What's this?"

The King looked at the strange object. "I don't know. It must have dropped out of the sky."

"Maybe it's a clue."

"Or a necklace for a lady with a very fat neck. Or maybe

it's a very thin, humongous bagel." The King was full of good ideas.

"A bagel?" asked the Prince, looking at the King.

"Yes, what do you think?"

While the men in the Royal Search Party discussed bagels, the Queen stared at this vaguely familiar object and tried to remember where she had seen it before. But she couldn't. It was just on the tip of her brain, so to speak.

"Yes," she shouted finally, "give me that thing." And she snatched it out of their hands. "It's Mr. Snake!"

Prince Dropoffsky was surprised at this behavior and pulled the King to one side. "I think she's lost it."

"The bagel?"

"No, her mind."

The Queen was overjoyed. "Yes, look, you see he has swallowed his tail. It's definitely Mr. Snake."

"Perhaps she's a closet herpetologist," suggest the Prince.

"I don't think so."

The Queen held Mr. Snake up like a telephone and talked to him as if she had a bad connection.

"HELLO, MR. SNAKE. ARE YOU THERE? CAN YOU HEAR ME?"

"Hissy, hissy."

"OKAY, GOOD. THIS IS OLIVIA'S MOTHER. OLIVIA'S MOTHER," she shouted, even louder. "OH, FINE THANKS, HOW ARE YOU?"

"Hissy, hissy."

"OH, SHE'S FINE BUT WE'VE LOST HER. DO YOU HAVE ANY IDEA WHERE SHE MIGHT BE?"

"Hissy, hissy."

The Prince had never seen anything like this. "Has she ever done any snake-charming?"

"Not around the house."

"Did she ever tell you that she was a snake-charmer?"

"No, but I never asked."

"DO WHAT?" she shouted. "LOOK INTO THE FOREST? WHAT FOR? WE'VE ALREADY DONE THAT! BESIDES, I DON'T LIKE IT OUT THERE."

"Does she have any snake friends?"

"No, I'm sure she doesn't." The King was confident about this. If she had snake friends he certainly would know about it. They were quite close and shared things like that.

"BUT WHY, MR. SNAKE, WHAT GOOD WOULD IT DO? I DON'T UNDERSTAND."

"Hissy, hissy, hissy, hissy."

"OH, I SEE! WELL, IN THAT CASE."

And so, finally, she walked a few steps into the trees, followed closely by the King and the Prince. And, POW! There was Olivia, jumping up and down as high as the ceiling of her putrid cage would let her.

There were several moments of general, joyous jubilation. Everyone joined Olivia and jumped up and down enthusiastically.

"I found her, I found her," cried the Prince, "I knew I would, my nose never fails me."

"I'm sorry, Prince Dropoffsky," said the Queen, passing Mr. Snake back to Olivia through the bars of her cage, "but *I* was the one who found her."

The King rushed over to Olivia. "Olivia, my Precious, my Darling Daughter, my Only, my Goodness, thank Goodness, Good Gracious . . ." He babbled on incoherently.

"Olivia," said the Queen, "what are you doing in that filthy cage. Come out at once!"

Olivia pointed to her mouth and shook her finger back and forth.

The Prince asked, "Are you Princess Olivia, a long-lost maiden?"

She nodded that, yes, she was.

"Good," he said proudly. This solved the first part of his curse. Before he could give her the letter he had for her, she held up her hand to hush them and laid her pointer-finger across her lips.

"I think she wants us to be quiet," said the Prince.

"What on earth for, out here in the middle of the forest? Tell us, Child! Don't be so mysterious! Speak up!"

Olivia pointed to her mouth and shook her finger again.

"What does she want?"

"Is this another of your little games, Olivia?"

Olivia shook her head.

"Maybe she can't talk," said the Prince.

"YOU CAN'T TALK?" asked the Queen, thinking that if she couldn't talk she probably couldn't hear very well either. Olivia nodded. "WHY NOT? EXPLAIN YOURSELF! Oh, she's up to her old tricks again. This won't do at all. I DEMAND AN EXPLANATION!"

Olivia held up her hands again until they were quiet, and then reached through the bars of the cage, took the padlock in her left hand, and looked at them as if she were asking a question.

"Yes," said the Prince as though he were talking to a child. "Padlock. Pad. Lock." She nodded. He was getting the idea. Then she twisted her pointer-finger around back and forth like a key, in front of the padlock.

"Pencil sharpener!" said the Prince, who loved charades.

She shook her head and then, very carefully, pointed to the key hanging on the end of the cart handle just out of reach, and said with her lips, "Key. Get the key." But they didn't see this because they were watching her hands.

So she tried the padlock again. She put her pointer-finger in front of the padlock and twisted it around. With her mouth she formed the word *key* and made, as you must, if you say the word with enough gusto, a very big smile. "*KEY.*" But this, both the word and the smile, were lost on the Royal Search Party.

"Screwdriver?" suggested the Prince. She shook her head. After this she didn't know what to do so she pointed again to the key hanging in plain sight.

"She's pointing at something."

"What could it be?"

"She's pointing this way."

"Is it something in the forest?"

"Is it a wild animal?"

To these questions she nodded or shook her head and occasionally rolled her eyes.

"Is it bigger than a bread box?"

"Is it made of metal?"

"Is it small?" These were good questions and she began to have hope, but they were soon off again in the wrong direction.

"Does it eat meat?"

"Will it bite me?"

"Does it sleep at night?"

"Is it used for something?" asked the Queen.

Olivia nodded.

"What's it used for?"

She pointed to her mouth and shook her finger.

"Oh, yes, I forgot."

Finally, she pointed at the Prince, who said, "Me?" She nodded and then put out her palm and walked her fingers across it. "Walk," he said. She nodded again. Then she pointed toward the key. Then, before he had taken two steps, she threw up her hands and he stopped. Then she pointed to her eyes. "Eyes," he said, and she nodded vigorously. Then, using her fingers like eye beams, she bent over and looked down, and poor Dropoffsky also looked down but didn't see anything but his boots and a few forest ferns that had been badly trod upon. Then she tapped her finger on the handle of the cart and slid her fingers along it and—and—and—FINALLY he got the idea.

"Oh," he said, "the key, why didn't you say so?" She put her hands on top of her head and said to herself, "Please, please, preserve me from idiots like this."

"Aha! This is the key to the padlock. Just as I suspected." He was so pleased that he had figured this out all on his own that it wasn't until Olivia waved at him again and pointed at the padlock that he finally put the key in and opened it.

At that very instant Count Carlos, who was hiding in the dark, leaped out like an immense toad, knocked Prince Dropoff-sky to the forest floor, and sat on him. Georgette was smiling her beautiful smile because she liked a bit of action and was ready to help if needed.

The Royal Couple were shocked and stood with their mouths open. Olivia shook her fist at the Count.

"NOT SO FAST, LITTLE PRINCE-BOY," shouted the Count. "Give me that key."

But the Prince was quick and managed to roll over onto his stomach and hide the key with his fist. "You can't have it!"

"GIVE ME THE KEY BEFORE I TOSS YOU INTO THE SWAMP!"

"I won't. Finders keepers, losers weepers."

"FINDERS SCHMINDERS, LOSERS SCHMOOZ-ERS."

"Get off me, you big oaf. Hey, what are you doing?"

The Count was in the process of twisting off his left arm. "I'M GOING TO TAKE YOU APART LIMB BY LIMB!"

"You don't scare me a bit." From this you can see that, among many other admirable traits, the Prince was brave.

"GIVE ME THE KEY!"

"No."

"YOU WILL!"

"I won't."

"YOU MUST!"

"I mustn't!"

"GIVE ME THE KEY BEFORE I DO SOMETHING EGREGIOUS!"

Even with the terrible weight of Count Carlos on his back, Prince Dropoffsky squirmed about, freed his right arm, and, with a quick motion, tossed the key to the King, who, of course, wasn't expecting it. The key, an old-fashioned, rather heavy item, bounced off his chest and fell on the forest floor. By the time Count Carlos got off the back of the Prince and scurried over to the King, the King had tossed the key to the Queen, who also wasn't expecting it, but was able to juggle it about for a bit, and then catch it just in time to toss it over the Count's head back to the King. By this time Dropoffsky was on his feet, and a frantic game of keep-away ensued with the Count, as the monkey-in-the-middle, running back and forth among them shouting at each in turn. They even tossed it once, by mistake, to Georgette, and she, without thinking, tossed it right back to them. Count Carlos was in a rage but couldn't stop to yell at her.

He shouted about and raced back and forth in his pot-bellied manner, grunting, panting, cursing, and leaping frantically into the air, like a pig playing volleyball. I mean, talk about exercise! By now, they were surrounded by a large group of fuzzy, furry, forest friends, whose curiosity had overcome their timidity. They were enjoying the sport, laying a few side bets on whom they thought would win, nothing large, you know, just an acorn or two. They were clearly for the home team although they weren't entirely sure who the home team was. They laughed and cheered when the Count fell down, or missed an easy chance of grabbing the key, and screamed wildly when the Prince tossed it to the King under his leg in an ostentatious, but brilliant, display of bravado.

The Count was soon tired and stood in the middle, panting, facing the Prince, who waved the key in front of him to irritate him. He huffed and puffed and threatened to blow someone's house down. The tension mounted, and our forest friends were transfixed, barely breathing. Even the noisiest little creature sat silently, watching, hushed.

Suddenly the Count lunged at the Prince, who tossed the

key again to the King, but the Count vaulted high into the air and touched the key with his pointer-finger, knocking it out of its trajectory, over the cart, and into a bed of lichen and moss.

Olivia watched it go over her head and pointed to where it had landed for the Prince and the Royal Couple as they came around the ends of the cart. Unfortunately, the Count was too quick for them. He executed a spectacular headlong belly-whacker in the mud and slid under the cart with his arm extended and grabbed the key before the others could get there. In one muddy hand he had the key and with the other he removed a fern frond that had become lodged between his teeth.

"FINALLY! FINALLY!" he sputtered, spitting out a few dandelions, but by the time he got his fat body out from under the cart, no easy task since he was out of breath, the Royal Search Party had fled for their lives. Only a few fluttering leaves and a trampled jack-in-the-pulpit indicated which way they had gone.

"WAIT!" he shouted after them. "WAIT! WHAT ABOUT THE RANSOM? Now what am I supposed to do?"

"Perhaps I may be of service, my Liege," said Georgette, always ready to help.

"Yes. Yes, you can."

"What may I do, Sir?"

"After them, my Pet, and bring them back to me."

"I'll fly by night, I'll fly by day,
Across the sea, across the bay,
Where'er thou wilt, where'er thou say,
I'll do thy bid at work or play."

"What is that, Shakespeare?"

"No, my Liege, but my work is oft compared to that of the Bard."

"Look! We don't have time for literary discussions. Here's what I want you to do. Quickly, quickly, follow them through the forest and bring them back to me so that I can get them to pay the ransom. After them, my Pet, after them!"

But instead of leaving, she struck a lovely pose.

"I'm gone with the breeze,
Through forest and bog.
I hope I don't freeze,
Or get lost in the fog."

"Would you just get on with it, without all the stupid poetry?"

"Yes, SIR." She saluted and was off in a flash.

Count Carlos paced up and down. Princess Olivia watched

him with dark looks of disgust and contempt, to which he paid no attention whatsoever.

"She'll be back with them in a minute," he said, "and I will squeeze the King like a bunch of grapes until gold oozes out of him like sugar from a maple tree. And then I'll tell him that he doesn't really need all that money anyway. And then I'll say something like 'Free, fry, fro, from' just to scare him. Or maybe I'll say, 'Excuse me, Murgatroyd, your slip is showing,' just to confuse him and make him nervous. And then, if he still doesn't come across, I'll tell him all the terrible things I'm going to do to you, his darling daughter. Such as, well, I suppose I could start by catching a few rats and putting them in the cage with you and letting them nibble their food from between your toes. Yes. It will be fun to watch you dance around and scream. Heh, heh, heh. And then, of course, if he really doesn't want to pay the ransom, I can start cutting your hair off, all jiggy-jaggy. That would be amusing. And, if he totally refuses flat-out, I will start sticking you with porcupine quills, except that I use rusty nails instead, they work quicker. And then there's the rack. Maybe I'll get Georgette to build a monstrous rack and I'll make you about ten feet tall and even skinnier than you are now, and I'll call you 'Mozzarella' just for the fun of it. What else shall I do to you, my Pretty? You always have lots of ideas."

Olivia pointed to her mouth and shook her finger.

"Oh, yes, I forgot. You can't talk, but you're a very good listener. Heh. Heh. Heh." He laughed his joyless laugh and sat down on a stump to wait.

Princess Olivia was furious and disappointed. "How can I help my parents now," she said to herself, "if this nasty Count keeps me locked in this filthy cage and threatens to do all those terrible things to me. What can I do? What can I do?"

Chapter Ten

Count Carlos sat on his haunches, poked at the fire with a stick, and waited for Georgette to return with the Royal Search Party.

"When this is all over," he said, "I'll put them all in the cart and exhibit them at the Tunbridge World's Fair as a ROYAL FREAK SHOW. I'll give them rags to wear and chain them together and make up evil stories about them." He was beginning to drool, thinking about how he could insult them whenever he felt like it because they would be right there in his cart. Then he heard Georgette's voice in the forest.

"LEFT! LEFT! LEFT, HAW, LEFT!" She marched the King, the Queen, and the Prince in like soldiers. "Company, HALT! One, TWO! Right FACE!" She walked up to each one until her nose was one inch away and stared into their eyes with a snarl on her pretty face. "YOU! Stand up straight! YOU! Chin

up, shoulders back! YOU! Tummy in! Okay, that's more like it."
Then she turned to the Count and smiled her angelic smile and
blinked her blazing blue eyes. "There you are, my Liege."

"Thank you, my Pet."

> *"No sooner said than done,*
> *No sooner done than said,*
> *First we'll have a honey bun,*
> *And then we'll all to bed."*

"Well done, well done, but next time, NIX THE POETRY!
IT'S TERRIBLE!"

> *"All my poetry is good—or bad,*
> *Or upside-down, or just a fad."*

He glared at her and said,

> *"Tweedle-dee and Tweedle-dum,*
> *Here is one that's just as dumb."*

"My Liege—you can do it! You can make verses!"
"Of course I can, anyone can. BUT I DON'T WANT TO!"

"You're a poet,
And don't know it.
But your feet show it,
They're long fellows."

She laughed for several minutes at her new joke. Her face got red and she had to cover her mouth to keep flies out, but the Count didn't see anything funny about it.

The Royal Search Party stood shoulder-to-shoulder at attention, expecting the worst. Count Carlos strutted over to his prisoners, flush with power and arrogance. He stabbed his pointer-finger into the King's chest.

"ARE YOU, OR ARE YOU NOT, THE KING?"

"I am." He tried to sound brave, but his voice quivered.

"AND IS THIS, OR IS THIS NOT, YOUR DAUGH-TER?" He pointed dramatically to Olivia.

"She is." He knew that honesty was the best policy.

"AND IS SHE, OR IS SHE NOT, A PRINCESS?"

"She is."

"AND IS SHE, OR IS SHE NOT, LOST?"

"Lost?" said the King, brightening up, "Oh, no. She was lost, but we've found her, don't you know. The Prince helped us. We've been up all night, but we found her, right here in the middle of the forest."

Count Carlos couldn't imagine how anyone could be so abnormally stupid. "Well, isn't that nice?" he sneered.

"Yes, thank you, it is. We're very pleased, as you can imagine. We were really quite worried, especially her mother."

"But, you're not worried about her anymore?"

"No, why should we be? She's right over there, and, if you don't mind my saying so, in the pink of health."

"Don't you realize that SHE'S LOCKED IN A CAGE?"

"I had noticed that, actually. Probably some game she is playing. She loves games."

"IT'S NOT A GAME! SHE'S IN THAT CAGE BECAUSE I PUT HER THERE, AND I'VE GOT THE KEY!" He waved the key in the King's face.

"Why is she in the cage?"

"BECAUSE I PUT HER THERE!"

"And you have the key?"

"YES! HOW MANY TIMES DO I HAVE TO TELL YOU?"

"Well, then, you'll let her out, won't you? There's a good chap."

"Of course, old Chap—AS SOON AS YOU GIVE ME A GAZILLION DOLLARS!"

"Oh, I see," said the King, weakly. Now, for the first time, he understood the situation.

Count Carlos was wild with frustration. "Didn't you read the ransom note?"

"I—I—I skimmed it."

Noble Prince Dropoffsky came to his rescue and spoke up with authority, taking command of the situation.

"I read the ransom note, Count Carlos, and I'm afraid that you have made a grievous mistake. You have completely forgotten something." He crossed his arms imperiously and looked over the Count's shoulder into the forest.

"Is that right, little Prince-Boy? What exactly have I completely forgotten?"

"The King cannot pay."

"Would it be asking too much, little Prince-Boy, to ask why the King can't pay?"

"No, it wouldn't."

Count Carlos waited for the Prince to speak, but he didn't, he just kept staring into the forest. "Well, why, then?"

"Because he's here."

"So?"

"So he's not in his countinghouse, counting out his money."

"What difference does that make?"

"And, not only that, but the Queen is not in the parlor eating bread and honey."

"Bread and honey?" The Count was flummoxed. "What does eating bread and honey have to do with anything?"

"Allow me to explain," said the Prince, now that he sensed the Count's inferior intellect. "This is a situation where even a smattering of knowledge of the great field of poetry would have been helpful to you. Unfortunately, your categorical rejection of the subject constrains you to the ignominious institution of ignorance."

"What on earth are you talking about? I don't want to talk about poetry. I HATE POETRY!"

"Precisely! Your negative response ratifies my contention that you are an ignoramus."

"What I am, or am not, has nothing to do with the case. HE MUST PAY THE RANSOM! I DEMAND THAT HE PAY THE RANSOM!"

"He can't pay the ransom."

"HE MUST PAY THE RANSOM!"

"He can't pay the ransom."

"HE MUST PAY THE RANSOM!" His nostrils flared with fury.

At this point, the King tapped the Prince lightly on the shoulder. "Excuse me, Prince Dropoffsky, but actually, I can pay the ransom. I have my checkbook right here. I carry it with me everywhere."

This extraordinary offer to write a check was an idea that had occurred to the King with no consultation with his wife, who was standing speechless, appalled that he should say such a thing. Under the circumstances, his idea was a clever one. He knew that he had no dollars and no cents in the bank and that if he wrote a check, it would bounce like a red, rubber ball, high up in the sky. And he was counting on the Count not to know anything about accounts, checks, banks, tellers, deposit slips, or any of those other complicated financial thingamadoodles. Ordinarily, the King wouldn't do something like this, he was an honest person in every way, but this was a special occasion. The evil Count had his daughter locked in a cage and was going to keep her there until the ransom was paid.

"YES!" said the Count, "MONEY!" He pumped his fist like he had won a tennis match, saliva formed at the corners of his mouth, and the King knew at once that he had fooled the Count.

But the Prince didn't. "Put that checkbook away," he said to the King, giving him a poke.

"Well, there's no need to be rude," he said with mock irritation to further confuse the Count.

"YOU KEEP OUT OF THIS, LITTLE PRINCE-BOY, OR I'LL SOCK YOU IN THE KISSER." He then turned pleasantly back to the King. "Now then, where were we?"

"I was just getting ready to write you a bounce—I mean a check."

"Yes, good. Just make it out to Count Carlos M. von Dusseldorf. Dusseldorf, with two *s*'s."

By this time the Queen realized that her husband was giving away their entire fortune, having momentarily forgotten that they didn't have a fortune. She thought that her dear Horace had lost the rest of his mind.

"Don't write that man a check, he may cash it!"

"Not to worry, my dear, it's only a gazillion dollars."

"It's not the money, it's the principle of the thing. He's a bad man, I can tell by the way he smells and his looks."

"Actually, I think he looks a little like your cousin Agnes."

"He does not! How can you say such a thing?"

"WOULD YOU JUST KEEP OUT OF THIS!" The Count was old-fashioned and thought that women had no business in business, especially in complicated, highfalutin negotiations such as these.

"I have a right to express myself. It's a free country."

"When you talk like that," said the Count, "you remind me of someone. Oh, yeah—HER!" He pointed his crooked pointer-finger at Olivia, who stuck out her tongue at him. "But never mind all that, just make that check out for a gazillion dollars and stop wasting time."

"How many zeros in a gazillion."

"I don't know, about fifty, it doesn't matter, they're just zeros."

So the King wrote out a check while Count Carlos peered over his shoulder, and while he was filling in the countless zeros the King asked him a friendly question. "What on earth are you going to do with all this money?"

"I'm gonna buy me a little pizza place and hire a pretty girl to make pizza. Did you ever see a pretty girl making pizza?"

"Can't say as I have."

"It's a sight to see. Now go ahead and sign that baby."

The King prepared himself for the signing of the Royal Check, which was always something of a production because he did it with such grandeur and flourish. But then he hesitated.

"SIGN IT!" Count Carlos grabbed him by the collar and twisted it.

"DON'T SIGN IT!" his wife shrieked. "DON'T LET HIM MAKE YOU!"

"I think . . ."

"SIGN IT!"

"DON'T SIGN IT!"

"My wife doesn't think it's a good . . ."

"SIGN IT!"

"DON'T SIGN IT! WE'LL BE POOR FOR THE REST OF OUR LIVES."

"My wife . . ."

"SIGN THAT CHECK BEFORE I TIE YOUR KNICKERS IN A KNOT!"

"How would that help?"

"DON'T ASK SO MANY STUPID QUESTIONS."

"DON'T SIGN IT!"

"What you don't seem to realize is that my wife . . ."

"SIGN IT!"

"Perhaps we could discuss this somewhere in a more relaxed atmosphere, perhaps over a cup of tea."

"SIGN IT!"

At this point the Queen, who was standing in front of the Count, did a complete 360-degree turn like a discus thrower and smashed the Count upside his head with

her flashlight, and suddenly they were all fighting. With one hand she prevented the King from signing the check and with the other she banged away at the Count's head using her flashlight like a hammer. The Count had the King by the collar and, at the same time, fended off Prince Dropoffsky who had taken hold of one of his legs and wouldn't let go. The King could barely be seen behind all the fighting that swirled around him.

Finally, Georgette, who until this moment was enjoying the fray, decided that things were getting out of hand and leaped out in front of them.

> *"Alakazoo, alakazam,*
> *Stay where you are,*
> *stay where you am.*
> *I'll thank you, Ma'am,*
> *and I'll thank you, Sir,*
> *To——slow——right——down——and——do——not——stir."*

It was as if all their batteries went dead at the same time, and they were frozen in a most extraordinary tableau.

"Well, now, looky there! Not bad, if I say so myself." Georgette put her fists on her hips, smiled, and shook her head in disgust. "This is a sorry sight. Grown-ups! What are they good for?"

While she untangled them she sang a little song that went like this:

"Here's a really sorry sight,
They ought to be ashamed,
The Count would like to fight all night,
I think he's lost his brain.
His eyeballs both are popping out,
With all-consuming greed,
He jumps and shouts and bangs about,
A needy man indeed.

"Your father, alas, he dithers about,
Not knowing what to do,
It's hard to fight when you've got the gout,
It's bound to make you blue.

"And Old Mother Hubbard protecting the house,
Her castle is her home,
Not a creature was stirring, not even a mouse,
Not even a dusty gnome.

"And our Hero is gasping for air like a fish,
Like a fish, on the beach, out of water,
It doesn't seem likely he'll get his wish,
To go back home like he oughter.

"So there they are, a sorry sight,
An angry motley crew.
How bad it is to shout and fight
If people only knew."

When she had them sorted out and standing in a row, unable to move or speak, looking like children who had misbehaved, she said, "There. That's better, isn't it?"

But Olivia still couldn't speak because of the spell that was on her. And with all this fighting, she was no closer to helping her parents than before. In fact, quite the opposite!

Chapter *Eleven*

When Georgette saw Princess Olivia waving to her, she said, "Oh, yes, I forgot." Assuming a special pose, she wiggled her fingers as was required to uncast a spell.

"Sucoh-sucop," she said, and then whispered to Olivia, "That's *Hocus-pocus* backward."

> *"Sucoh-sucop, I'm such a dope,*
> *But do not weep.*
> *I'll make the spell go up in smoke,*
> *And you shall speak!"*

A small puff of smoke appeared at the ends of her fingers.

"Oh, thank you." Olivia's voice rang out clearly in the forest air. "Thank you. I didn't realize how much I like to talk. Oh, yes, it's wonderful. Now I can tell you how I'm feeling and how worried I was when they were fighting, and—and—oh, now I've forgotten what I wanted to say. Oh, yes, I don't think it was very nice of you to say those things about my mother and father."

"But I got them to stop fighting, didn't I?"

"Yes, that was very good. Very skillful! It doesn't hurt them, does it?"

"They won't remember a thing."

"Won't Count Carlos be mad at you?"

"I'll make him think he's been at a sumptuous luncheon with smothered this and fricasseed that." She patted the old Grouch on his tummy, and he smiled and licked his chops.

"Georgette?"

"Yes."

"Now that old Greedy-Grumpy is unavailable for comment, why don't you open the gate to this nasty cage and let me out of here?"

"I can't think of anything I would rather do, but I can't. If I did, I'd be in serious hot water when old Greedy-Grumpy woke up."

"What would he do?"

"He would put my magic hat on his own fat head and turn me back into a bronze statue, and, oh—anything but that!"

"He could do that?"

"Oh, yes, he could. He used to do it a lot, but now all he has to say is the word *bronze*, which sends chills down my spine, and I do whatever he wants." She shuddered charmingly from the chills she had sent down her own spine.

For Olivia, however, this small fact, the fact that the Count could do magic if he had the hat on his head, was very important, critical information. It occurred to her that if he could do it, so could she. She immediately had a scheme—a brilliant scheme to free her and help her parents, and, of course, the Prince, since he had been so kind and helpful.

While Georgette was inspecting the Royal Search Party, Olivia told her scheme to Mr. Snake, who listened carefully. "What do you think?" she asked.

"Hissy, hissy."

"You'll do it, but you want me to do something for you in return? Later?"

"Hissy, hissy, hissy, hissy."

"Oh, I see. Of course. I should have thought of that a long time ago."

So then, with his permission, she picked him up casually and held him out toward Georgette. "Have you met my friend Mr. Snake?" she asked innocently.

"That's a snake?"

"Yes, and he's my friend."

"What's wrong with him? He looks like a circle."

"Yes, he swallowed his tail and can't talk very loudly."

"He talks?" Even Georgette had never seen a talking snake.
"Yes."

"And he's a friend of yours?"

"Yes, he's my best friend."

"Can I pet him?"

"He doesn't like to be petted but he loves to be twirled around."

"Twirled around?"

"Yes, here, just put him around your waist and wiggle your hips. He loves it." So she passed Mr. Snake out through the bars of her cage, and Georgette had him spinning around in a jiffy.

"Like this?" Needless to say, she looked splendid spinning Mr. Snake around, her supple form bending this way and that like a rubber tree in a tropical breeze, all effortless charm and grace.

"Good. You're very good at it. Now follow him wherever he goes. Wonderful! Faster! Faster!" Why did Olivia encourage her? Was Georgette going to turn into butter? Was she going to fly over the moon? What was going to happen? What was Mr. Snake going to do?

Olivia watched and waited, and then, when Mr. Snake brought Georgette close to the cage, she reached out and snatched the magic hat off her head, and in an instant—POW!—Georgette was a bronze statue with a blank face. Not just an ordinary bronze statue, of course, but a very beautiful one with an extraordinarily lovely, poignantly expressive, blank face.

"It'll be all right," Olivia said to her friend, "you'll see." This was more a hope than a promise, because she didn't know if the hat would work on her head, and if it didn't—then what?

"Thank you, Mr. Snake, you did your part and now I'll do mine." She picked him up and held his head in one hand and his tail in the other. "This may hurt," she warned.

"Hissy, hissy."

"Do it quickly? You mean like when you take off a bandage?"

"Hissy."

"Okay, here goes." She gave a quick yank.

Poor Mr. Snake winced, then coughed a few times, and then he straightened himself out, stretched this way and that, and said in a deep voice, "Thank you, Princess Olivia, you're very kind."

"You're welcome!" She was glad to be helping someone at last.

"Now then," she said, looking at the hat, "first, I have to

put it on." This wasn't as easy as putting on a ball cap, for example, because she wasn't sure which was the top, and when she had what she thought was the top on top, the sides didn't look like sides, they looked more like bottoms. Finally, she got it on and hoped it looked becoming although she wasn't sure because there was no mirror anywhere about.

"Now then, let's see. Somehow, I have to get out of this stupid cage." She had never tried to do magic before, so everything she did was an experiment. She held the padlock in both hands and said, "Open up." She pulled at it but nothing happened. "Open up, please," she said, remembering that her mother insisted on politeness for every occasion. But again, nothing happened. Then she tried, "Hocus-pocus, please open up," and "Hocus-pocus, please open up, Sir," and "Hocus-pocus, Alacazam, please open up, Sir," and many other variations using the words she had heard Georgette use. She wiggled her fingers and crouched down, then crouched down and wiggled her fingers. Nothing worked!

"Maybe I should try some verse. Yes, maybe some little poems will do the trick." She took time to think. Making verses is not easy.

"Hocus-pocus, do not blunder," she said. "That's a good first line, but then what? Let's see, what rhymes with *blunder*? Um. Um. *Plunder. Sunder. Thunder*? Yes, maybe *thunder*. Let's see.

"Hocus-pocus, do not blunder,
Give us now a blast of thunder."

BOOM, Boom, boomidy, boom, boom, boomidy, boom, rolled across the sky.

"Yes," she squealed, "I did it!" Then she said,

"Louder, louder, if you please,
I can do this thing with ease."

KABOOM, KABOOM, Boom, boomidy, boom, boom, came from a sky now black with clouds. Rain washed down on her like cats and dogs, as they say.

"Heavens to Betsy, rain! Mother was right after all. Let's see." Quickly, she came up with another one.

"Rain, rain, go away,
But please come back another day."

POOF!—The sun came out again all bright and shiny. The plants and the trees, and the furry, funny, forest friends wondered what had happened. A short thunderstorm was to be expected once in a while, but this was ridiculous.

Now that she had the hang of it, she turned her attention to the padlock.

Charles F. D. Egbert

"Abracadabra! Open sees me!
You'll do as I say and soon set me free."

The padlock answered with a small, gentle, but very much appreciated *click*, and, with no trouble at all, she slipped it out of the hasp, opened the door, and stepped out of the stench of the cart down onto the soft, green, clean, tender, loving ground, making sure that her little hat didn't get knocked off.

This, for the young Princess, was a new world. Now she was in charge. Now she could do anything. She had amazing new power—power at her fingertips, everyone's dream.

Immediately she turned her attention to the beautiful bronze statue standing next to the cart.

"As for you, my crepe suzette,
You'll no longer be Georgette,
But, Diane, my little sister, be,
We'll dance and sing and climb a tree."

"Oh, look what you've done. You've made me into your little sister. Thank you, Olivia, I always wanted to be a little sister." She clapped her hands. "We'll dance and sing and run and play."

"Yes, and toast marshmallows and play flutes and listen to *The Wind in the Willows.*"

"Oh, boy!"

"But first, I have to take care of Mother," Olivia said. She was a good girl who took her responsibilities seriously.

> *"Mother mine, Oh, Mother, dear,*
> *Bestir yourself, and be of cheer,*
> *And do not order me about,*
> *And make up rules for me to flout."*

The Queen blinked several times and yawned. "Oh, my. What happened? I must have fallen asleep." She looked rested and cheery. "Olivia, how nice you look. And who is this lovely young friend of yours?"

"This is Diane, Mother, my little sister."

"How nice to meet you, Diane."

"It's very nice to meet you too—Mother!"

"Mother? I'm your mother?"

"Yes, because she's my sister." The logic was impeccable, so the Queen brushed aside her doubts, thinking that this pretty but unknown child might be hers. Perhaps one she had forgotten about, in the headlong rush of life. She forgot all sorts of things. But now it didn't matter. Gone were her former scolding, her faultfinding, and her pointing out the dangers lurking in the gray corners of life. Now she saw Olivia as the person she really was, warts and all. This is just an expression, of course, Olivia didn't have warts—no heroine does—it's not the tradition.

"And now I must help Father." Her father was still standing where Georgette had put him, staring dumbly into space and clutching his checkbook as though it were a small creature trying to escape.

> *"Your checkbook, Dad, was almost bust,*
> *But now has changed and grown robust,*
> *With lots for you, it's only just,*
> *And as for me, I'll have a trust."*

The King opened one eye and looked around carefully before he opened the other. Then he straightened the collar that Count Carlos had twisted out of shape, checked that his checkbook was in hand, pulled his robes about him, and spoke to Olivia.

"My checkbook, you say?" He looked at the new, very substantial numbers and said, "Well, look at that! Yes, yes, just as it should be." He took this immense windfall in stride—good news is remarkably easy to get used to. He didn't even pry into it, he just accepted it.

The Queen looked at the new balance. "Oh, my goodness,

how nice. Now we can get those Royal Drapes I've been wanting, and have some slipcovers made for the thrones. We'll have the counting room done over, and buy some bubble-bath."

"And I can get some new shoes."

"Don't forget food."

"Oh, yes, I agree, food. We definitely need food. Most definitely!"

"And my hair," she said, throwing up her hands, "something must be done about my hair." This was not one of the King's pressing concerns since he didn't have any to speak of.

"And Olivia needs a new sweater."

"This will be very good, we'll have a new life."

"Yes, we will. Thank you, Olivia."

"You're welcome."

"Thanks a million," said the King, who, now that he had something positive to think about, wasn't bothered so much by his toe.

Diane pulled gently at her sleeve. "What about old Grouchface?"

"Just watch," Olivia said with ever-growing confidence.

> *"Carlos Maximillian, I decree,*
> *You shall my humble butler be,*

And carry out my every wish,
To fetch a ball or catch a fish."

The Count had trouble coming back to life. It started in his feet with small, jumpy, little spasms, like bubbles at the bottom of a pot just before the water boils. Then he had a few knee jerks, which led directly to serious twitching in his fat upper body that sent his arms and hands out violently in sundry directions and made his head bobble-dobble around like one of those toys that can be seen on the dashboards of other people's cars. It was several minutes before he could bring himself to accept the idea of being someone's butler, but finally, his new-self won out over his old-self. He calmed down, straightened his back until he was practically bending over backward, drew his face up into an expression of significant, almost insolent, imperturbability, and looked way down his nose to speak to her. "Perhaps, Mamzelle would care for a glass of lemonade."

Olivia clapped her hands together. "How nice! Not now, but maybe later, Binkerton."

"Would Mamzelle care for anything at present?"

"Yes, thank you for asking, Binkerton. My shoelace, I'm afraid it's a bit loose." She put her foot out prettily.

"At once, Your Highness." He knelt in front of her and tied the lace gently.

"*Your Highness* is a nice touch, Binkerton."

"Thank you."

"Thank *you*, Binkerton."

And now only Prince Dropoffsky was left.

> *"And you, sweet Prince of Royal Blood,*
> *Shall rise again and stem the flood,*
> *Of sluggish rivers, oozing mud,*
> *This precious youth shall grow and bud."*

I'm not sure why, perhaps it was because he was young, but the Prince was awake in an instant and looked at her quizzically, hardly recognizing her, since she was so different from the cringing, cowering creature he had seen in Count Carlos's crummy cage only moments earlier.

"Are you Princess Olivia?"

"Yes, I am."

"Aha! Just as I suspected." The Prince hadn't really changed very much, but then, why should he? "I have a letter for you."

"Just imagine!" she said. It was the last thing in the world that she expected.

He took the envelope from his bag and handed it to her. She was very excited. Everyone, even Binkerton, gathered around while she opened it.

"It's some sort of official document," she said as she opened it. "'To Whom It May Concern,'" she read. "'If you are now, or ever have been, a Lost Maiden, please sign below.' Yes, of course." She took Prince Dropoffsky's pen and signed.

"What else does it say?" asked the Prince, looking over her shoulder.

"'When you have signed this document, please give it to Prince Dropoffsky, who is probably looking over your shoulder right now as you read this. He will have to get Count Carlos to sign as well and then he will be free of my curse. Sincerely yours, the Sorceress. PS. I'm sorry for any inconvenience I may have caused.' And look, here's a place for him to sign as well. Binkerton!"

"Yes, Mamzelle."

"You need to sign this paper."

"Sign, Mamzelle?"

"Yes. Just sign Count Carlos M. von Dusseldorf. Dusseldorf, with two *s*'s."

"But, Mamzelle, I thought I was Binkerton."

"Just sign it, Binkerton!"

"Yes, Mamzelle. As you wish." He signed the document and gave it back to her, and she, in turn, gave it to the Prince.

"Now I'm free and can return to the Ompompanoosuc River Valley, save my impoverished people, and resume my Royal Life as a Prince once again. And get rid of these ridiculous shorts."

"I like them." Shorts on men with shapely legs were a weakness of the Queen's.

"Wait," said Olivia and held her hand up.

> *"And one more favor,*
> *If thou canst,*
> *The Prince wants back,*
> *His Royal Pants."*

POW! They appeared just like that. They looked new and, I might add, very impressive—velvet with darts on the sides, slished and slashed about with artistic abandon, and below the knees, he had spotless white stockings and pointy Royal Slippers on his feet. He was clearly pleased with how he looked and turned at an angle, so that everyone could admire him. The brown shorts, to the Queen's disappointment, were now a thing of the past.

"It is my Duty, Princess Olivia, my Pleasure, and my Honor to lead you back safely to the castle."

"In those ridiculous slippers," she said. "I think we can do better than that." Obviously, mucking back through the forest and swamp the way they had come was out of the question for these now wealthy members of the uppermost class.

> *"Again, my little hat, please help us,*
> *We need your gentle art.*
> *And to the castle's hearth, please take us,*
> *Upon a magic carp."*

A beautiful carpet that was blue like the sea with gold fish jumping out of it, just like the one in their drawing room at the castle, glided to their feet, barely rustling the leaves.

Binkerton helped the ladies onto the magic carpet, and followed behind the Royal Gentlemen, when they had boarded. They sat in proper rows and Binkerton went up and down the aisle checking to see that they had fastened their seat belts, especially Mr. Snake, for whom the belt was way too big. Take-off was smooth and before they knew it, they were standing on the drawing room carpet that had been, just a few seconds before, a magic carpet. They were all delighted to be indoors again and out of the weather.

> *Olivia got their attention.*
> *"Of all of my wishes, I'll make this the last,*

Charles F. D. Egbert

Please give us a feast,
A glorious repast.

"From pancakes and bacon, we'll no longer fast,
We'll eat and we'll eat,
See how long we can last."

No sooner had she said this than they heard a muffled clamor in the Royal Dining Room with the clatter of dishes and the clinking of glasses. Binkerton, who was now warming up to his role as a butler, announced the Royal Breakfast.

"SOUP'S ON," he cried.

"No, no, Binkerton, that won't do at all. You must say, 'Dinner is served, Your Highnesses.'"

"Beg pardon, Mamzelle?"

"You must say, 'Dinner is served, Your Highnesses.'"

"Yes, Mamzelle. Dinerzerveyurinesses."

"But wait, before we go in to eat," she said.

"Thank you, thank you, little Hat,
For doing what I wish like that,
And since your tasks are nearly through,
And I have no more work for you,

You now can go and sail on high,
And we can say a fond good-bye."

She threw the hat into the air, and everyone cheered, and the hat, loyal to the last, flew out of the window and soared higher and higher into the sky until they could no longer see it and everyone waved and cheered.

There was a Royal Grand Procession into the Grand Dining Room. The King and Queen went first, looking splendid considering that they had been up all night and hadn't been able to change their socks or take a shower. Prince Dropoffsky followed them, in his new velvet trousers, with Princess Olivia on one arm and Princess Diane on the other. "This is more like it," he mumbled to himself, looking first at one pretty girl and then the other.

In the dining room they were met with a roar of welcome from the townspeople who somehow had gotten wind of their return and had managed to wangle invitations. They were all present, Hope Sew's entire family, Ezekiel Washtubs, Mary Antoinette, Mr. and Mrs. Baker, and Mr. Atwood who offered a toast to Princess Olivia: "Here's lookin' at you, Kid."

"Here, here," they all shouted, except Hope's brother Ignorance, who said, "There, there."

The tables were set with sunflowers and beeswax candlesticks, and the dishes were made right there in Ipswich by the Potter family. Binkerton lorded over the waiters as they brought in one splendid dish after another. First there were pancakes and waffles with maple syrup, and then corn chowder, puff-ball soufflés, potatoes from Pomfret, cheddar soup, slices of wild turkey, fresh fillet of trout, and buttered acorn squash. And then, for dessert, there was ice cream, fried dough, peaches and pears and cheeses of all sorts, with Common Crackers, and apple pies, and apple brown Betty, blueberry cobblers, and blackberry fool with custard on top, and thin slices of pear, and dandelion and sassafras tea, and that was just the tip of the iceberg. Each dish was met with shouts of "Bravo," or "I say, look at that," or "Aha!" and "Just as I suspected."

The King made a speech and gave toasts to everyone's health and prosperity, and to the new lives that they would all have. He spoke with elegance about what they could do now that they were out from under the cloud of the terrible Count Carlos Maximillian von Dusseldorf. He would bring the villagers to new levels of Civic Consciousness, Peaceful Patriotism, and Restful Responsibility. He would institute Annual Town Meetings, and Ox Pull Contests, give prizes every year for The Tallest Sunflower, The Biggest Pumpkin, The Best Heirloom Tomato, and The Best Goat, Pig, Cow, Horse, Rabbit, and Chicken. Thunderous applause greeted each of these announcements.

Everyone at the Royal Table talked about what the future held for them, especially the girls, who couldn't wait to get started.

"And, Prince Dropoffsky, what will you do now that you are no longer cursed?" the Queen inquired politely.

The Prince put down his napkin with youthful dignity. He had been completely absorbed in the two pretty girls across the table, how nice they looked, and how gleefully their imaginations romped over the meadows of the future.

"I will return to the Ompompanoosuc Valley and save my people, and the sooner I begin my journey the better." He rose from the table to shouts of "Oh, no," and "Don't leave," and "Why not stay for a while?" But he was determined.

He shook hands with the King and bowed deferentially to the Queen, who dabbed at her eyes with a hankie. He winked at Diane and then stood quietly in front of Princess Olivia. She wasn't sure what to do, so she put her hand out to shake, and the Prince took her little fingers, bent over, and kissed them tenderly. Olivia looked over at Diane with her eyebrows raised all the way to her bangs, and they broke into a chorus of smothered snorts and giggles.

Then he stood up and walked forth, across the bridge over

the moat, thonk, thonk, thonk—he had changed the Royal Slippers for the Royal Hiking Boots—and when he was on the other side, he turned and waved. "Good-bye. Someday, perhaps, I shall come here again and—and . . ." But he couldn't finish; he had a lump in his throat. He walked on, never turning to look back, down the hill and across the covered bridge, with the picture of Princess Olivia's smiling face painted forever on the back of his eyelids. "If only," he said to himself, "she were a little older."

The townspeople, with their tummies full, paid their respects to the Royal Family, bid them farewell, and went home. And Mr. Snake, who had stuffed himself as much as anyone, said in his wonderful deep voice, "Thanks for a good fill, Olivia. See you around," and slithered off gracefully in the direction of the bower.

When they had all gone, the Queen got up from the table announcing that there was a lot to do. The King agreed, and they set off briskly in opposite directions.

"I'm happy that I was able to help them after all."

"Yes, you did a great job," said Diane.

"What do you suppose will happen tomorrow?"

The End

Acknowledgments

My parents encouraged my imagination and introduced me to A.A. Milne, *Alice in Wonderland* and *The Wind in the Willows*. My sons Garth, Noah and Matthew were endlessly patient as I created characters, plots and new voices for their bedtime stories.

Olivia Dreifuss was the inspiration for *Princess Olivia* and my companion in make-believe as we spent endless mornings in the sunshine of a Vermont farmers' market. Her sense of humor and creativity were boundless. I wrote a short story about Olivia's ability as a world class hula hooper and rewrote it as a play – the original rendition of *Princess Olivia*. Prince Dropofsky and his wardrobe were inspired by Dave Yesman, a UPS driver and our first friend in Vermont.

After a reading of *Princess Olivia*, Don Velsey had the wizard idea to set the play to music. His melodies and lyrics and the cast of talented actors (including Kate Shaper as Princess Olivia; Justin Bendel as Count Carlos; Irna Skowronskia as Georgette; and Blair Howell, Linda Ide, and Larry Shaper) brought *Princess Olivia* to life on stage.

Thanks to fellow writers in the Hundred Pages Club who helped shepherd the play into a novel. My wife, Carol, who created a magical hat for Georgette and fanciful crowns for the king and queen in the story's first incarnation as a play, has been a helpful editor and a creative consultant every step along the way. Thanks to Ib and Carole Bellew, my publishers, who have been encouraging and supportive in the process of bringing the novel that once was a play to print. It has been a joy to work with them and Kathie Kelleher, whose illustrations echo the whimsy of the story.